NO HELL
BELOW US

A POLITICAL TOUR DE FARCE

by JOHN TWAIN

NO HELL BELOW US

Shimmer Tree Books

Copyright © 2023 by John Twain

First Shimmer Tree Books Edition

Paperback ISBN: 979-8-9864145-7-7

Published by Shimmer Tree Books, Shimmer Tree LLC

This book is dedicated to You, the kind of brilliant, charming, good-looking reader who leaves 5-star reviews and tells all your friends to check out *No Hell Below Us.*

NO HELL
BELOW US

1

A Devilish Idea

The World Demonic Forum opened with a few blasphemies, and then Satan started the formal proceedings.

"Murder—up this quarter. Debauchery—up. Adults and children being chemically and surgically mutilated due to 'transgenderism,'" he said with air quotes and a snicker. "Way up." An evil grin spread across his face. "Well done, Zyzyx."

Little blasts of flame and smoke arose from their hands as Satan and the demons applauded Zyzyx for his contribution to the suffering of humans, especially the young ones.

From this evil opening, the meeting trudged along, taking much time to accomplish little, as meetings do.

Satan was about to adjourn for lunch when Blyx lifted his hand. The demon was Züming in, as he was in the field trying to stir up a race war on another part of the planet.

His lips moved, but no one could hear what he was saying.

"You just muted yourself," said Zyzyx, covering his mouth and pointing at the screen in some kind of impromptu sign language. "We could hear you, but then you muted yourself," he said louder than needed with each word enunciated as if he was speaking to someone hard of hearing.

Blyx unmuted himself but then turned off his video. His voice sizzled through the speakers, though his face was replaced with a generic dual-horned avatar.

Satan slammed his fist into the table and erupted, "Turn your video on!"

"Sorry, I'm on my phone . . . always have trouble with these buttons on the app . . ."

Blyx appeared on the screen accompanied by his voice all at the same time to an irritated room of infernal spirits. "I have an idea . . ."

"Listen," Satan said. "Your 'race war' has been underwhelming. More of a race *spat* so far. What I need from you is less ideas, more hatred and death."

"But that's just it. I was out here stirring up resentment, bloodshed—the whole deal—when it hit me. Picture this," the demon said. He paused as if to give his audience time to brace themselves for the grand idea he was about to unleash upon them. No bracing occurred, as it was quite past lunchtime at this point, not to mention, demons are not known for their attention spans. Blyx continued, "You make the human race look like one race."

Satan sat back in his chair and put his hand on his forehead. He gave a sideways glance to Thad, his secretary. "What am I supposed to do with this guy?"

All the demons were yes-men to Satan's face, but Thad was obsequious to the bone. Well, he had no bones, but you know what I mean—idiomatically.

"You've considered banning him to the outer darkness before," Thad whispered. "Maybe now's the time."

"Hear me out, guys," said Blyx before he muted himself again. Once more through the mute, video off, both sound and video back on cycle, and he continued. "If we—"

"Is that even possible?" said Zyzyx. "To make all the humans one race?"

Now, Zyzyx had a good point. But as a demon, his motives were always evil. He was riding high on his transgenderism stunt, and he wasn't eager to lose the spotlight to some new idea out of left field. He understood the devilish power behind Blyx's suggestion the moment he said it. With modern humans, all disruptions, even a disruption seemingly in their favor, would be twisted by the most wicked among them toward a destructive end.

"No, Satan can't do that," said Slin. "Can't create. Can't change the physical world."

Now, nothing infuriated Satan more than hearing what he couldn't do. That's what got him into the whole damned mess he was in in the first place.

He sat up and moved just his eyes to view Blyx on the screen. There was no way he would end this otherwise triumphant meeting—triumphant from his perspective, at least—with himself looking as impotent as he truly was.

Satan stroked his chin, a sure sign he had surrendered to the idea. "*I am* in the details," he said. "It actually has potential. Reductionist evil. Reminds me of my early work in the Garden," he added, looking at Thad. "Put together a subcommittee to research the best means by which—"

"Uh, Satan." It was Blyx. "I don't mean to interrupt, but I got this one. You give the green light, I'll get it done, posthaste."

Satan didn't like that Blyx was showing himself to be clever and industrious, qualities which had long departed Satan himself. The chthonian underlord had been reduced to a rather unimaginative bureaucrat by this point in his career—surely part of his judgment. Not exactly a lake of fire, yet a sign that the end was nigh.

But the die had been cast ages ago. So, he did what heads of bureaucracies do—hedged his bets to maximize credit for himself should the results be destructive and minimize blame if failure (in this case, goodness) resulted.

"We'll put it to a vote. No guts, no ignominy, boys."

Against their better judgment, each demon said, "Aye," as Satan's gaze locked in with their own, taking part in the eventual blame for what was surely, in their minds, a venture destined for doom—well, doom in the sense that they thought it would fail, not that it would actually lead to doom, which would be success from their perspective, of course.

"Fine," said Satan. "Thad, send Blyx the appropriate paperwork, then blast out the objective in . . . um, that new protocol we used for 'Project Family Friendly Drag Show' . . ."

"WhatsUpp, sir," said Thad.

"Right, alert the organization via WhatsUpp. And you," he said, turning his face to the screen, "this is on you, Blyx. I'm giving you board-approved authority on this machination. Don't mess up."

Thad pressed a button on a remote control, ending their Züm with Blyx.

The demons nervously eyed each other over this decision. Sure, their latest projects had been calamitous for humanity, but there had been failures, too, over the years. Satanic Metal, which turned out to be too on the nose; man buns—embarrassing, but not devastating; and many other interventions with bad intentions that did not produce the cataclysms they hoped for.

The tension in the room quickly dispelled as lunch arrived on ivory-trimmed platters—meatless soy steaks and kale with no dressing, a demon favorite.

2

Yay?

"What a . . . momentous . . . um . . . event," said Raven DiCherubino, speaking on live television from zer* mansion in the Hollywood Hills. Zhe tried to smile, but zer lips quivered at the edges, making zer look like zhe had just been handed a sweaty sock. "Yay," zhe said, with a delivery that sounded more like a question than a statement.

As co-founder of Colorful People Count, Mx. Raven DiCherubino was asked to address the world on SNN (Spin News Network), or at least to that part of the world forced to watch SNN while waiting for a flight in the airport.

It was only twenty-four hours ago that one of the oddest phenomena in human history occurred—all people, in nearly an instant, were transformed into a single race.

James, a black man in Idaho, went to sleep with the same physical features he had known all thirty years of his

---

*Mx. Raven DiCherubino's Handy Dandy Personal Pronoun Guide can be found on page 161.

life. When he woke up, his skin was a new shade, the average of all human skin tones. His face was subtly different, too—it had shifted to a sort of generic blend of male features. Same with his hair. Yet, as he stared in the mirror in shock, he still somehow looked like himself. Something in his eyes.

The same thing, but the female version, happened to Daisy, a white woman in New York, and Vivian, an Asian woman in Georgia.

This transformation happened across the nation. And in South America and in Asia and Africa. And to all people on all continents—even the scientists in Antarctica, who at the time were using a fifty-million-dollar grant from the US government to develop a Pride flag that could withstand the extreme weather of Climate Change™. They stopped watching their very cold flag whip in the polar wind and looked at each other in amazement. They were all . . . one race.

• • •

A few short years earlier, Raven DiCherubino was trying to make it big as a social justice street performer and failing miserably. Zhe called zer one-person act "The Anti-Minstrel Minstrel Show," in which zhe claimed that zer own show, featuring zer donning blackface, was proof that white supremacy was alive and well in America.

One night after an especially disheartening performance on the Venice Beach Boardwalk to an audience of one neo-Nazi, who wasn't there for the irony of her show, zhe first set eyes on Abraham "Abe" Z'Bendy, B.S. (he always insisted that people include his Bachelor of Science in kinesiology degree as part of his title when referring to him). Z'Bendy performed a pantomime using his hands and exaggerated facial expressions to recreate the mime cliché of the man in an ever-shrinking box. He stood on a crate labeled "fossil fuels" and his black shirt proclaimed in white block letters, "Climate Change™ is Crushing Me!" He then acted out the *Communist Manifesto* from cover to cover, impressively, DiCherubino thought, given that he used no words.

As he got to the part of the *Communist Manifesto* about the abolition of private property, a homeless man got a little too close to his tip jar, and Z'Bendy handily shoved him aside without skipping a beat in his muted storytelling. DiCherubino admired Z'Bendy's prioritization of theory over people. *He gets it,* zhe thought.

After closing his act with a solo performance of the Soviet National Anthem in International Sign Language, DiCherubino approached and asked him if he would join zer on a walk. Z'Bendy used his index fingers to draw his frown into a smile, then made that heart-shaped deal with his hands over his chest, and the two walked off together.

As they sat on the shore of the Pacific Ocean to watch the sunset, Z'Bendy discovered he had just been poked by a dirty hypodermic needle in the sand. He made the crying mime face and pointed to it. When DiCherubino reached down, gently removed the used drug paraphernalia, and tossed it away toward a nearby swing set, Z'Bendy knew that he had met his soulmate.

Z'Bendy broke his silence to thank DiCherubino, and the two talked into the night—the sound of crashing waves, as well as the cacophony of an off-beat drum circle populated by intoxicated homeless men, providing the score to their conversation.

"It's just not fair," said DiCherubino. "It was so fun hating those overt racists of the past—the ones who said they were racist and then backed it up by behaving in a discriminatory fashion toward those of other races."

"They don't make 'em like they used to," said Z'Bendy with a sigh. He pulled a partially eaten soft pretzel out of his pocket, broke off a piece, and squirted some mustard on it from a plastic packet. He dropped the plastic packet in the sand below and handed the pretzel bite to DiCherubino.

Zhe put the bite in zer mouth and chewed while looking Z'Bendy in the eyes. "There are no great battles left. Well, the use of fossil fuels to improve the quality of life for billions of people, increase the human lifespan dramatically, and reduce world hunger—Xi mean, it's pretty fun fighting against that. But setting xyxelf up as a warrior against racism, in a time in which racism is universally opposed by all decent people—that's challenging. It's so hard to find . . . good old-fashioned racists anymore."

"True," said Z'Bendy. "There will always be racism, but people of different races seem to be getting along better and better over time. I mean, look at us—me, a black man in pantomime whiteface and you, a white woman in blackface—talking on the beach, and no one even gives us a funny look. What do we have to do to get attention?"

"Right?" said DiCherubino. "It's maddening!"

Z'Bendy handed the rest of his pretzel to DiCherubino. He watched as zhe ran zer finger along the winding curves of the salty pastry.

"That's it!" Z'Bendy snapped his fingers. "I've been developing a new critical theory called Pretzel Logic, and you helped me see what was missing." He reached over to the pretzel and traced its twisting curve as he spoke. "When someone has ideas that differ from our ideas, we will use pretzel logic to show that they are actually espousing . . ."

And then, as if by romantic magic, they spoke in unison: "Racist ideas!"

"Yes," said DiCherubino, whose face lit up brighter than the time zhe came across a vintage issue of *The Daily Worker* at a thrift shop.

Z'Bendy stood up, rubbing the spot where the hypodermic needle pierced his skin and was quickly growing an infection. "And, if they suggest that free enterprise or families or Christianity or correct answers in math or *Leave it to Beaver* or anything else we don't like is good, we will say they are promoting white . . ."

"Supremacy," they said together.

"But," DiCherubino continued, "people are so frustrating. If we start claiming we see racism and white supremacy everywhere we look, they will want . . . evidence and stuff."

Z'Bendy pinched off a piece of the pretzel in DiCherubino's hand and took a bite. He spoke as he chewed on the doughy bread. "Got it," he said. "We'll say unequal representation or outcomes in any human activity—business, academia, entertainment, square dances, hockey, whatever—are the result of white supremacy."

"But, what about something like a professional sports team that has mostly black players?"

"That you would bring that up, Raven, is proof of your promotion of *whiteness*," he said with disgust.

DiCherubino's eyes opened wide. "But, Xi was just—"

"See what I did right there?" Z'Bendy said with a smile.

DiCherubino had a greedily lustful look in zer eye. "Xi would ravish you right now . . . but Xi had my genitalia removed because of an idea Xi had that my gender and sex didn't line up, and therefore, if Xi removed my sex organs, Xi would be a more complete person."

"Me, too!" said gender-fluid Z'Bendy as he embraced DiCherubino in an impotent hug.

The waves crashed behind the two eunuchs as the drunken drummers played on in the distance.

• • •

DiCherubino and Z'Bendy got busy crafting a plan to generate more racism to hate, and then to monetize that hate using capitalism to usher in communism to make the world a better place for themselves. Z'Bendy was the brains of the operation, elaborating on his initial Pretzel Logic critical theory; DiCherubino was the blunt force that bullied people into supporting their mission.

Their first book, *White Inferiority*, raced to the top of the bestseller's lists as elite white people in the media gave gushing reviews of the book that smeared regular ol' everyday white people's character. The cover of the book featured the faces of its authors, Z'Bendy right-side up, DiCherubino upside down—they decided the pantomime and minstrel looks they wore when they met were great branding, so they kept that—which created a sort of highly insulting yin-yang symbol.

By the time their follow-up smash hit, *Man, White People Suck!*, landed in bookstores, Z'Bendy and DiCherubino were the darlings of SNN and earned tens of thousands of dollars per appearance on the elementary school speaking circuit, where they scolded kindergarteners for perpetuating racial hierarchies in their sandbox play. In addition to payment of their speaking fees, to be made in small denomination cash in recyclable shopping bags, their contracts stipulated that a basket of freshly baked pretzels and plastic mustard packets be provided to them, as they enjoyed reminiscing about their humble start that fateful night on the needle-littered California beach.

It wasn't long before labeling everyone they disagreed with as racists and convincing millions of people that all white people (except for Raven DiCherubino) were white supremacists actually started causing more racism. DiCherubino and Z'Bendy were thrilled. "At this rate," DiCherubino said in private, "we'll be back to legalized slavery in no time at all, and then we can pretend to be abolitionists!"

And then it happened. The at-the-time President of the United States, Ace MacDonald, was caught on a hot mic saying that "Ebony and Ivory" by Paul McCartney and featuring Stevie Wonder was only his second favorite song of all time—behind "I Think I Love You," by the Partridge Family.

DiCherubino and Z'Bendy personally despised the song and its promotion of racial harmony, but they knew they could twist MacDonald's admission into his gut like a dagger. They held a rally at Pooch's Beer Hall in Poughkeepsie, New York, to denounce MacDonald's hate speech about the classic 80s hit and demand that Congress impeach him immediately.

They were joined onstage by Moe Stealinette Hyden. Hyden was a former Used Car Salesman of the Month at Big Al's Car Shack and current challenger of MacDonald for the presidency. DiCherubino and Z'Bendy weaseled into the leadership of his campaign, seeing that he was suffering from dementia, which made him easy to control. Plus, they noticed he had no values whatsoever—so he was a perfect vessel for DiCherubino's and Z'Bendy's ideology.

Hyden grabbed the mic. "When I was a child, I wanted to sell snake oil. But my mama told me, 'Moe, the elixir you need is not to be found in the skin of serpents but in politics, but I repeat myself.' True story, man. No, I'm serious. True story, man. No, I'm serious." He got stuck in a loop, so Z'Bendy walked up and gave him a good whack on the back. "You know, folks, back in my day, I would've challenged Ace to a thumb-wrestling match down by the ol' water tower and won—would'a done it. But that's not how we settle things today, see. Today, we settle things by going to a little club I like to call the 'After Hours Vote Counting Speakeasy,' and that club don't open till the Republicans go home for the night . . ."

DiCherubino elbowed Z'Bendy, who sprang into action and tried to get the mic from Hyden. "No, I'm serious. True story, Jack. But, in closing, let me say, as-salamu alaykum and goo goo g'joob."

Z'Bendy then stood on a table, and after a long, dramatic silence, led the audience in a chant: "Colorful People Count!"

It was an otherwise boring summer, as Americans had, until recently, been forced to remain indoors by the government to avoid chemtrails released into the air by the government. So, when audio from the DiCherubino-Z'Bendy-Hyden event leaked, the pent-up left-wingers of the US erupted into violence. The right-wingers would have joined them, but there was a *Dirty Harry* film festival on TV at the time.

DiCherubino and Z'Bendy registered ColorfulPeopleCount.com, started a non-profit, and asked wealthy, elite, white people to send them money so they could increase the number of things they label as racist, and, more importantly, so they could lobby

Congress to officially declare "Ebony and Ivory" America's new National Anthem.

To thank DiCherubino and Z'Bendy for causing billions of dollars in damage to their businesses from looting, CEOs of every major corporation sent multi-million-dollar checks to Colorful People Count to show that they, too, think "Ebony and Ivory" should be the new National Anthem.

DiCherubino and Z'Bendy thrilled as celebrities, business magnates, politicians, and regular citizens replaced their own profile pictures on Fluttyr with the DiCherubino-Z'Bendy yin-yang symbol, which became the logo of Colorful People Count.

And oh, how they danced to Rage Against the Machine, toasting each other with stale pretzels and cheap mustard as the money rolled in and America burned.

3

Follow the Science

But how did it happen? you ask. *You're not just gonna skip over how all people became one race, are you?*

Take it easy. I was getting to that . . .

So, Blyx was playing the long game. Let's not forget, as a demon, he'd been around for a long time. He watched Satan grow complacent as the leader of their cursed endeavor, often just letting humans do what they do and then taking credit—or worse yet, following their lead.

Global Warming Alarmism. That one was all on the humans. Blyx remembered when Satan brushed that idea off when it first started brewing. "Boring," he said as he focused on influencing rock musicians to put backward messages in their songs—boy, did he get a kick out of that—wore out more than one needle on his turntable playing records in reverse hoping to hear mention of himself. "Plus," he argued, regarding Global Warming, "people won't fall for it. I mean, what about ice ages and warming periods before human fossil fuel use? They know about all that. And the *sun? Hello.* They're dumb, but they're not that dumb." Flash forward to when Global Warming became Climate Change™, the ultimate tautological twist, and Satan claimed he had invented the whole thing.

And then a few years ago, he demanded that all the demons refer to him as Satynx, part of his rebranding of himself as trans after seeing Zyzyx's idea take off like wildfire with teenage girls and autogynephilic men. It never really caught on in the demonic realm since spirits aren't sexual beings, so the demons had to all pretend it never happened.

But Blyx was patiently biding his time all along—pretty much since the fallen angels fell.

He built up a network of demons who would interact with humans in the realm of science—well, astrology at first, and then alchemy, but eventually, actual science once the dreaded Christians invented the Scientific Method.

Blyx started with three demons. He had them infiltrate the dreams of three scientists and then each was expected to recruit and train at least three more demons to do the same. "It's not a pyramid scheme," he assured each one as they stacked up underneath him, the sole architect and power broker at the top of what definitely operated like a pyramid.

The method was simple. Demons can't interact with the physical world beyond a couple spiritual parlor tricks, like slamming a door in a creepy house or nudging a person here and there. For them, it's all about influencing humans. So, once Blyx had a network of several thousand demons interacting with as many scientists, they were able to collect and connect knowledge with an impressive level of efficiency. The real key to staying ahead of the humans was due to an unforced error by the humans. They limited the development of knowledge by elevating certain scientists and discoveries based on that which supported the power structure of the elites; that which challenged the elites was stifled. The demons drew from the elite scientists but also from those who never saw a dime of grant money, those who toiled away in their basements obsessed with the physical nature of reality. It was actually from the latter that the demons stole the best ideas.

Blyx studied this knowledge—about organisms and DNA and chemistry and energy fields.

He called on his top lieutenants to, from the legions of scientists they controlled, find out who the three dumbest ones of the bunch were. "Make sure they are true pseudoscientists," he told them, "empty, vain tools into whom we can pour pure evil and they will call it good."

Blyx was so thrilled with the low quality of humans his lieutenants brought to him that each was rewarded with a pink Cadillac—well, a spiritual version of a pink Cadillac, which was more like a smoky salmon-colored aura they could float around in—this made the other demons in Blyx's organization unbearably jealous.

The first "scientist" was Octavia Adoncia-Cervantes, or OAC as she preferred to be called. OAC got her start as a biologist by receiving a scholarship to an online science college, the award for winning a hot dog eating contest on Coney Island. The headquarters of the science college was on "Native land," so instead of teaching modern science, the school promoted pre-Scientific Revolution beliefs about nature. They were at the time the nation's leading experts on trepanation as well as leech-based treatments for stubborn belly fat.

The second was a chemist, Blaze Eppy. *Not* a federal agent, this provocateur's claim to fame was the time he encouraged—though did not directly participate in—the storming of a Starbanks Coffee Shop that ran out of oat milk. It was dubbed "Dark Sunday" by the media due to the failure of the company to order enough of the nectar of the millennials (oat milk, that is), which forced these otherwise well-mannered citizens to drink black coffee—and to superglue their hands to bags of dark roast and weep bitterly of their oppression. Oddly enough, though he fired up the crowd that launched this protest, Eppy was the only individual involved to receive a gift card for a free beverage from the coffee giant, while those he led were politely told to consider almond milk or to come back on Monday.

And finally, the demons selected Michelangelo Von Cappuccino. Though Von Cappuccino was one of the most critically acclaimed actors in Hollywood at the time, he was equally well known for his obsession to develop a faster private jet so he could more quickly shuttle girlfriends off his private island when they forgot to refer to him by his preferred adjectives, "lusty" and "zesty." He claimed that his experience portraying a scam artist who impersonated a physicist in one of his movies qualified him to be a physicist in real life. He further bolstered his claim by touting the honorary doctorate he received from his acting school, though it was not in physics, of course. He was rarely photographed in public without his tam, the eight-sided mortarboard pillow hat Ph.D. recipients wear at graduations.

"There will be a special place in hell for these nitwits," Blyx hissed in delight.

It was devilishly simple from there.

Inspire Eppy, in a dream, to contact the other two and invite them to a conference for three in Putz, Switzerland.

Von Cappuccino was upset that he had to land his private jet in Davos, and then travel by limousine to Putz, because the limousine was not electric, and therefore contributed to Climate Change™. He was also annoyed that he had to bring his own servants, as Putz, being a small town, didn't have such accessories for rent.

The three demonic stooges sat in their motel's hot tub sipping kombucha and talking about sciencey stuff: like how boys can be girls and how science can mutilate them to prove it; that science thrives most when politicians determine which scientific proclamations are to be promoted and then social media companies ban all alternative views; and how scientists need to weaponize and release more infectious and deadly viruses so they can then develop new medical technologies to help people think they are safe.

OAC picked through some fresh fruit in a floating buffet tray. She made pouty lips. "Aw, no hot dogs."

"Let's get into why I called you both here," Eppy said, his breath visible in the chilly fall air. "It is time to implement the 'Envision Protocol' we discussed on the phone." They named their mission after "Envision," the melodically pleasing but philosophically dystopian John

Beetle anthem about a world devoid of morality, eternity, property, and meaning.

Not being a federal agent, Eppy had many connections in the FBI and CIA, as well as British, Russian, Chinese, and Panamanian intelligence (few realized how well spy messages on scrolls could be hidden in bananas, which made Panama a hotbed for cloak and dagger activities)— as well as to their various labs and technologies.

The GIHN (Global Institute of Health and Nihilism), located in Xingjiang, China, and secretly run by US Public Health Czar Timmy Fazi, was one of these Deep State-controlled labs.

While trying to figure out how to transform the bacteria found in human stomachs from healthy to deadly—so they could better understand how to cure their new deadlier bacteria through costly, experimental pharmaceuticals to help people—the GIHN came across an unusual discovery. Tweaking a specific gut bacteria protein in one of their "volunteer" Uyghur test-subjects triggered a change in his melanin, which, in turn, affected his skin color.

Eppy traded a pair of khaki pants and some aviator glasses for a detailed report of these findings from one of his fed buddies involved with GIHN operations.

Blyx then flooded Eppy's dreams and imagination with other melanin-based research from other labs, elite and basement, from around the world. Combining this extensive knowledge, Eppy understood how to manipulate that gut bacteria to select for any desired melanin level.

OAC was too incompetent to infiltrate labs the way Eppy did, so Blyx had to feed all the needed information to her directly. "*I'm Daaaarwin,*" he would say in a mysterious, ghosty voice, appearing to the "biologist" in her dreams. He taught her, in very simple, step-by-step lessons, often accompanied by cartoon-looking graphics, how to genetically tweak facial features and hair in humans using a blast of several frequencies of energy for a specific duration of time. OAC, of course, had no clue that Darwin lived and died prior to the emergence of the modern field of genetics.

So, at this point, Eppy and OAC understood how to adjust the skin color, facial features, and hair of humans. But the problem of how to apply these changes to all humans would be resolved by Von Cappuccino. Well, the words would come out of his mouth, though every principle and idea was planted in his mind by Blyx, and that, in turn, was produced by the work and demonic influence of countless scientists.

"We implement phase one of the Envision Protocol," the actor said, brushing the tassel from his tam out of his face, "by hacking Wardenclyffe and sending an electronic pulse around the world."

"Ah, Wardenclyffe," said OAC, pretending to know what Wardenclyffe was to sound smart, while Von Cappuccino insultingly clicked his tongue to get the attention of one of his servants for a refill of his kombucha.

Wardenclyffe Tower was created by the great scientist Nicola Tesla to carry out wireless energy transmission.

Supposedly, the project was never completed, and the tower, located in Long Island, was destroyed in 1917. It was true that the project was not completed at the time. However, far from being destroyed, the tower was carefully disassembled and then reassembled at a secret location. Using designs confiscated from Tesla's home by Deep State operatives after the genius's death, engineers were able to complete that tower and then make a duplicate. The two towers were erected at the North and South Poles, effectively turning the Earth into a giant energy broadcasting electromagnet. Satan managed this project and planned to use the Wardenclyffe Towers to send out what he called a "brown wave," a frequency that would cause the people of the Earth to lose bowel control all at the same time. This was on a dare from Zyzyx, but the silly and only slightly evil plan was on hold until after the November midterm elections in the US—Satan didn't want to risk the Progressocrats getting blamed for the stunt and consequently losing seats in the House.

Satan kept Blyx out of the loop on this one. Blyx didn't want to risk asking Satan for access to Wardenclyffe and getting denied, so he had Anonymous, the hacker, crack the code to enter the towers' mainframes. Anonymous was not a collective as many thought, but it was actually one guy, Willy, who could type really fast. "Easiest hack ever," the hacktivist chuckled to himself as he hit enter after typing "edisonsucks," deducing the password based on his knowledge that Tesla and Edison were bitter rivals.

And now, Von Cappuccino typed the same letters into his phone.

Thousands of miles away, twin towers came to life, transmission wires aglow, awaiting further directions.

Eppy grabbed a banana from the floating buffet tray and peeled it. He removed a small scroll from inside the fruit and read a series of numbers to Von Cappuccino, who in turn entered the numbers in his phone. The code represented frequencies and timing for the electronic pulses that were to be emitted from the towers.

Invisible beams blasted away from the towers in all directions, forming an interconnecting blanket of energy that covered the earth and extended about three hundred miles above the planet—just to make sure the astronauts at the two active space stations in orbit did not miss out on the experience.

Von Cappuccino raised his glass of kombucha. As Eppy and OAC did the same, three arms with skin of identical hue dripped above the bubbling water of the hot tub. They looked at each other's faces, their eyes wide in astonishment.

OAC wept tears of joy. "We did it," she said and then began singing the lyrics to "We Are the World."

Eppy shook his head. "'Envision.' 'Envision' is our theme song."

"Right," she said, clumsily shifting to a mashup of lyrics and off-key melodies from both songs. Her volume slowly decreased in an awkward fade-out to silence.

"To utopia," Von Cappuccino said with smug certainty. Glasses clinked and kombucha was guzzled as the three reveled in how they had just remedied one of the world's great problems.

And hovering above them, a host of demons, arranged in a pyramid with Blyx at the top, cackled in wicked delight at the destruction they had just seeded.

4

The Cocky Crowe

"It's been one month since we all became one race, and the theories are flying," said Panderson Blasé, SNN host of the nightly news broadcast called "Big Stories" or "BS" for short. "We have two of President Hyden's top advisors, Raven DiCherubino and Abe Z'Bendy, B.S., to offer some insights. Has the Hyden Administration found out what or who caused this bizarre racial shift that's apparently here to stay? What do you think, Mx. DiCherubino?"

"You just nearly genocided me by misgendering my second person pronoun, which is . . ." DiCherubino held up a card with the symbols "πü≈" written on it in her own blood, fingerprint style, and made an accompanying gagging sound, the verbal representation of the symbols. ". . . But since it is unpronounceable in English, I'll ignore your slight."

Abe Z'Bendy, B.S., who occupied one of the other talking head squares on the screen, spoke from another room in the Colorful People Count mansion. "I think I can offer insight into this, Panderson. Yes, the fact that humans are now all apparently one race does seem like a . . . wonderful reality," he nearly choked on the words, "but who is behind this? Using pretzel logic, it seems clear that this is the work of white supremacists who have manipulated people's skin to make it all one color that is not white in an effort to insert whiteness into the unfolding melanin-based hierarchy, with the ultimate goal of maintaining the status quo as dictated by whiteology."

"Interesting," said Panderson. "So, what does this mean for Colorful People Count? Do . . . all people count now?"

DiCherubino let out a dismissive huff. "Absolutely not, Panderson. Now more than ever, ze need to stand strong in what divides zux—maybe it's not race for now, but there are plenty of other things that can unite zux in hate against others. There is inequity. And let'x not forget men. They might not be white men anymore, but they're still . . . *men*," she said with a grimace.

"What about trans men?"

"Well, they're heroic by their existence, Panderson. But regular males who know they're men—they're the vestigial organs of society. And what do you do with a vestigial organ, let'x say an impacted wisdom tooth? Extract it and toss it in the trash," zhe said, making a ripping motion with zer hand.

"Well, speaking of standing strong in what divides us—"

"That's *zux*. You must use xy various personal pronouns when Xi am included in your collective context."

"Oh, of course," said Panderson with a most serious tone, "we . . . *uh*, ze will now be cutting live to the White House for a message from President Hyden."

Hyden had been selected President in "the most free and fair election in all of eternity," as the media described it, after MacDonald's impeachment and conviction for hate speech in what became known as "Ebony and Ivory-Gate." MacDonald tried his best to run a solid re-election campaign from his cell in GITMO, but the Islamic call to prayer played over the loudspeakers by the guards seemed to always *conveniently* align with MacDonald's press conferences.

Hyden was sworn in as President. Six months later, he declared a state of emergency and martial law after a group of Youth Scouts, none of whom, the President pointed out, were even on puberty blockers, picnicked too close to the fence surrounding the White House on the 4th of July. The media sprang into action, calling the unauthorized picnic an insurrection to justify Hyden's actions. The President's first executive order was to ban the 4th of July, which was removed from the calendar, much like 13th floors are not included in buildings.

Hyden spoke into a statue of a donkey on his desk in the Oval Office until an intern rushed over and redirected him to a microphone.

"Ah, yes," said Hyden, "just like my daddy always told me, talk to an ass, you'll get the horns. No, true story. I'm serious, man. No true story, I'm serious, man. No, true story . . ."

Panderson put his finger to his earpiece as the visual of Hyden froze into a fake pixelated "glitch" screen SNN created specifically to cover for Hyden when he went off-script, which was every time he addressed the nation.

"We've lost our transmission with the White House . . . again," said Panderson. "But, up next, we will explore the wonderful new development of 'Toddler Blockers,' drugs that allow infants to remain in a state of infancy, despite their age, so their parents can identify as 'new parents' indefinitely to get more attention. Our guest is Bill Cash, CEO of pharmaceutical giant, and also our number one sponsor, Gneuter Rx. What do you say to those who question whether Toddler Blockers are good for children?"

Cash looked into the camera. "Those who question this untested experimental drug, for which we cannot be sued due to collusion with the federal government, are Hitlerian ultramega Nazis who want the toddler suicide rate to skyrocket."

"Agreed," said Panderson.

•   •   •

Meanwhile, Ace MacDonald dictated his manifesto to his Gitmo cellmate, who scrawled every word on a roll of prison-issue toilet paper. Titled *My Struggle*, MacDonald laid out a new plan for America, which started with destroying his enemy, Moe Stealinette Hyden. His plan pretty much ended there, too, but he figured he would play the rest by ear once Hyden was removed from office, and he, Ace MacDonald, was restored to the presidency.

MacDonald was used to getting things his way through the sheer force of his will. He had made his first million hustling Membership Only jacket knockoffs in the 80s. Representing himself in court when he was sued for copying the iconic apparel's style, MacDonald made headlines in the fashion rags claiming that the snap on the Membership Only jacket's shoulder was cheap and low class. "Mine have buttons, gilded buttons," he said holding up one of his otherwise identical-looking jackets for the jury to see. "The button is a superior latching device. Tremendous attachment possibilities," he added, buttoning and unbuttoning the shoulder strap over and over again with a look of great confidence.

MacDonald won the case.

An early investment in designer leg warmers solidified his fortune, and by thirty years of age he was a billionaire titan of the fashion industry.

The "Ace" name began appearing everywhere as MacDonald mastered the art of branding—on Adopt-a-Highway signs, ballpoint pens included in every purchase of Ace-brand leg warmers, and banners on little league field fences across the nation.

There were some hiccups on his path to the top.

Several packs of Ace of Blades razors gave users tetanus after MacDonald got a deal on a batch of slightly rusty blades being sold out of the back of a truck in a big box store parking lot. When he saw that the judge in the resulting class action lawsuit had lockjaw, he knew he didn't stand a chance.

MacDonald's professional tiddlywink league never took off.

And "Ace Sings Tin Pan Alley" failed to chart, except in Liechtenstein, where it became a bestseller due to its popularity as a gag gift.

But Ace was resilient. He reinvented himself in Hollywood, creating and hosting the highly successful talk show *You Scratch My Back, I'll Scratch Yours.*

So, by the time he announced his bid for the presidency while ascending an elevator in one of his leg warmer stores, no one was surprised by his ambitious move. And though pundits acted shocked when he was actually elected, everyone knew: Ace never loses.

Yet here he was now. A convict. Sharing a cell with a guy he dubbed "The Scribe" (Ace never asked him his name), who was doing six hard for posting a meme with the caption, "Cis Genders Matter."

"Write this part in all caps, Scribe, to express my fury." MacDonald dictated: "I NEVER SHOULD HAVE ALLOWED THE PRESIDENTIAL ELECTION TO TAKE PLACE VIA A FLUTTYR POLL. ESPECIALLY CONSIDERING THAT FLUTTYR'S CEO AND HYDEN BOTH USE THE SAME DOG GROOMER, AS WE ALL WELL KNOW. THAT ONE'S ON ME, FOLKS. SHOULD HAVE SEEN THAT COMING. BUT IF YOU WANT TO KILL THE KING, YOU BETTER MAKE SURE THAT KING IS NOT ME."

MacDonald forged on, taking the first thousand squares of toilet paper to recount his accomplishments before getting to the point: He had dirt on Hyden.

Few were aware of MacDonald's and Hyden's history. Decades ago, they were presidents of competing *Welcome Back Kotter* fan clubs, which turned them into archenemies. They jockeyed hard to lure the actor who played the character "Epstein" to make an appearance at their annual Christmas party. MacDonald, of course, won that battle, though he was later pressured to disavow the entire *Welcome Back Kotter* TV show for its lack of diversity.

But the important thing is, it was during this battle that MacDonald learned of Hyden's weakness, well, his primary weakness: snow globes.

Those delightful orbicular wonderlands. Oh, how he would hold them in his hands in amazement as a child— the lead glass, the crudely crafted ceramic figurines, the bone chips masquerading as snowflakes swirling around stale water, all stirring his unusually dim imagination.

His collection began when he was gifted a set of snow globes from the uncle his family referred to as "the creepy one."

As a young man, he spent all expendable income he earned as a used car salesman to purchase rare snow globes.

As he matured, the themes of the snow globes he desired matched his evolving worldview.

At the time of his encounter with MacDonald, he had recently attained the first two of an ultra-rare three snow globe set: One featured Karl Marx holding a hammer in one hand and a sickle in the other with his foot on the neck of a worker; one had a statue of Charles Darwin hugging a monkey and winking. If only he could acquire the third, which displayed Sigmund Freud as a diapered baby, though still with a beard and cigar.

MacDonald paid one of Hyden's car dealership associates to steal the diary he took notes in at work—the kind with the clasp and lock that you could pick with a paperclip. The rest was easy as scooping up blank ballots from an old folks home on Election Day.

Mac Donald would never forget the look on Hyden's face when he beheld the snow globe in the poorly lit alley behind the used car dealership where he worked.

His arms lifted as if they had a will of their own.

"Not so fast, grabby," said MacDonald, whipping the globe back toward his chest.

"Be careful with it!"

"You got the letter?"

Hyden handed MacDonald a letter he had composed withdrawing his request that the *Welcome Back Kotter* co-star attend his Christmas party.

"Sign it," Mac Donald demanded.

Hyden signed the letter using MacDonald's back as a desk—that's how guys rolled back in the 70s.

MacDonald's face glowed in his victory as he walked off, folding and placing the letter in his coat pocket.

He looked over his shoulder, and what he saw was pitiful: A balding, middle-aged man holding a snow globe of Sigmund Freud as a baby as if it was a baby, caressing the glass and whispering, "My precious," over and over again.

Fast forward several decades. MacDonald heard rumors that Hyden was being influenced by unfriendly nations in the lead-up to the election he would eventually win. Powerful oligarchs in these nations were giving his son, Trapper, ultra-rare snow globes, ten percent of which eventually made their way to Hyden, whose code name in these corrupt operations was "The Big Cheese."

MacDonald tried to have the FBI and CIA dig up more details about the alleged corruption. "We work for the Left, President MacDonald," the heads of both organizations told him. "Haven't you even been paying attention?"

MacDonald was forced to send out his private attorney, Judy Ravioli, to get the goods.

"Track down the choicest snow globes on the Earth," MacDonald told her, "and there you'll find Hyden."

•   •   •

"My experience of life hasn't changed," said Flynn Crowe, speaking into a mic and looking at his hand. "My skin is lighter than it used to be. Face is slightly different. So what. I know a lot you are enjoying your new generic wavy brown hair. Well, I was bald before. Still bald. So, nothing new there for me. You'd think whoever or whatever averaged out our races coulda spread a little of the hair wealth around, too, while they were at it, but oh well.

"Stopped off for a coffee on the way to work. Had a pleasant exchange with the barista just like I did in the past, even though she used to be white. She was a little whiny before. Still a little whiny now. But it was all good. Same interacting with the man you all know and love . . ." Flynn shifted to a mock Japanese accent. ". . . Amateur wino and CEO of *The Cocky Crowe Show*, in a-second chair, Jerry San." It was off-color nicknames and even more off-color humor that led to continual warnings from *The Cocky Crowe's* adversarial platform, EgoTube. One more strike and the show would be canceled.

"I am half Asian, but I'm Korean. So it's just Jerry, thank you very much."

The show's producer clicked his keyboard and a huge comic book font "RACIST!" shook in front of Flynn's face as a pre-recorded broadcaster voice humorously boomed, "Racist!"

"I've always worn that smear as a badge of honor," said the provocative EgoTuber. His tone and face grew focused as he entered one of his serious monologues. "Just to be clear. Other than when it comes from our producer as part of a gag, the 'racist' label was always slung at me from a cynical person trying to soak up some power for themselves. I've been called a white supremacist because I think for myself and my ideas don't march in goose-step with the Left. The President's hack. What's that snake's name? The one that tools around with Abe Z'Bendy, B.S., on her arm like he's a cheap purse?"

"That would be Raven DiCherubino," said Jerry.

"Right. Raven DiCherubino called me the 'blackface of EgoTube' because I dared to call out her and Z'Bendy's corrupt front organization, Colorful People Count. I've also been called all the classic slurs for a black man by the so-called 'antiracists' who follow these two. But that's all over. There are no rac*es* anymore but one race. Personally, I think variety is the spice of life. But now we have, what?"

"Unirace?" said Jerry.

"Unirace. I liked being black, but I guess this'll work, too," he said looking at the skin on his arm and then grinning at Jerry. "And you look stunning in that skin color that is identical to mine and to every other human's on the Earth now. But the question is, what are the race hustlers gonna do? DiCherubino, Z'Bendy, the whole bunch. They must be heartbroken today."

Flynn put his hand to his headphones. "What's this? Let's go live to the White House for a statement from the Hyden Administration."

The producer hit a button on his computer and a low-fi video appeared on the screen. The heads of Hyden, DiCherubino, and Z'Bendy bobbling atop animated-looking bodies lip-syncing poorly to the old 60s song, "It's My Party," and sobbing as the lamenting lyrics describe.

"My apologies," Flynn said. "Wrong news feed. But seriously, enough with these lowlifes who use race to divide us for their own gain, though I'm sure they have something else nefarious up their collectivist sleeve."

The producer ran a scroll of audience comments from the show's live stream on the screen.

"Reading your comments, I see most of you are experiencing the same as I am—a bunch of life as usual. That's because—that's right folks—we're not racists. Now hit that like button. EgoTube—you can kiss my grits. Join Stein Gang to watch the rest of the show behind the paywall, where Jerry and I will be going toe-to-toe against each other in the game show you know and love, 'That's Sexist!'"

And indeed, Flynn's experience of the "Great Race Blender," as it became known, was the experience of the majority of people around the world.

There were a few holdout racists of various races who struggled at first to figure out who, of those they encountered, may have been of a different race than them prior to the unirace, but they soon grew bored of that and just stopped being jackasses, at least on that topic.

Most Americans were not racists in the leadup to The Great Race Blender. So, finding themselves and others to suddenly be of the same race, beyond their amazement with the whole phenomenon, changed nothing at all. They had already been living as if there was one human race.

But there was a third group, which included DiCherubino, Z'Bendy, Hyden, Panderson Blasé, and other powerful elites in government, academia, and media. This group referred to the unirace event as the "Yucky Race Erasure."

5

Klaven the Maven

Flynn Crowe and his wife, Dr. Jordache de la Roca, left their new production company's studio for a walk. They stopped to sit down on a grassy knoll not far from where President Kennedy was shot in Dallas, Texas.

"Did you watch that SNN clip of DiCherubino and Z'Bendy I sent you? They're really scrambling now that we're all the unirace."

"I'll tell you this—you ain't seen nothin' yet, man," said Jordache. "Some think they'll give up, take their ball, and go home. But it's like, no. They're not the kid that didn't get his way. They're the archetypal serpent backed into the corner of their own tiny, decrepit minds. Never cleaned their basements growing up, so now the Jungian shadow of the collective unconscious will rise up and do three things . . ."

Jordache paused to take a bite of her tuna fish. That's all she ate—a one hundred percent tuna fish diet, which she said helped reduce inflammation caused by the blue-haired critics of her and Flynn's work.

We better back up a bit . . .

Before The Great Race Blender, Jordache was a white woman. She earned her doctorate from and was a professor at Queenston University in New Jersey. The school originally had a totally misogynistic name that had been changed following a student-organized cry-in, which brought the trustees to their knees after about three minutes of tears. It was agreed that "Queenston" would be a good replacement name because it was more inclusive in that it excluded any reference to males in it.

Jordache had earned quite a reputation for herself due to her numerous published papers on psychopathology in pandas. She was a favorite of students because of her extensive knowledge and quick wit, but she also had integrity, which can lead to dire trouble in the modern university.

Shortly after The Great Race Blender, an omnisexual gender studies major started a post-modern power play at the Ivy League school. "It," as he preferred to be called, declared that "bananas are apples" and demanded that Queenston force all members of the university community to swear an oath affirming the same. It was an elite university, so the administration immediately caved and gathered the entire student body and staff for a mandatory rally. "Sometimes, one must simply drink the Kook-Aid," said Dr. J. Jones, Queenston's President. "And now, repeat after me—"

"Yeah. Not so fast, bucko," said Jordache, as she rose to her feet among the crowd. "I won't call your damned bananas apples."

"You are out of line!" shouted Jones. "Bananas are apples. And they always have been," he added, looking nervously at the gender studies student who stood next to him with its arms folded tightly over its artificial hormone-produced breast buds.

"Never before has Western Civilization failed to see the distinction between these two fruits, and you will not force my speech to the contrary now. Or ever. Who's with me?" Jordache said, waving her arm toward the mass of students and staff around her, many of whom had shared with her, in the lead-up to the oath-swearing ceremony, that they agreed with her one hundred percent.

Not a single person rose to join her. An otherwise insightful genius, Jordache forgot in that moment that the number one virtue in academia is cowardice—especially in the face of leftist demands that contradict truth, damage culture, and require the betrayal of friends.

"Guards, remove the infidel!" bellowed Jones from the stage.

Security emerged from the crowd and drug Jordache from the scene.

"Now, raise your hand like so," said Jones, lifting his right arm upward at a forty-five-degree angle from his shoulder, palm flat down, "and repeat after me. Bananas are apples!"

The thousands gathered raised their arms and said the words with a rather lackluster delivery.

The gender studies student shot Jones a steely glare.

"I can't hear you," shouted Jones, nervously cupping his hand to his ear. "Again. Bananas are apples!"

This time the crowd shouted the words.

"Bananas are apples!" he repeated, with passion.

And the crowd complied.

School representatives dumped tons of rotten bananas and apples on the ground. The masses screeched "bananas are apples" in an increasing tempo and intensity to the point of frenzy as they stomped them into one putrid cesspool of mutilated fruit.

Echoes of Jordache's words could be heard in the distance as she was shoved into a golf-cart security vehicle: "The Gulag Archipelago is calling—it wants its ethos back!"

Of course, Jordache was immediately fired from her professorship.

Back at her on-campus housing, she took to Fluttyr and flitted a meme of herself standing in her power-pinstripe suit, holding an overripe, limp banana between two fingers with a look of disgust on her face and a caption that read "Queenston—as American as Apple Pie"—and that was it. Queenston's gender studies undergrads launched torch apps on their smartphones, stormed De La Roca's home, tarred and feathered the once-beloved professor, and dumped her off at the crossroads that led out of the pastoral college town.

Jordache sat in the dirt, plucking feathers from her skin. "These kids didn't even have the competence to tar and feather me properly," she thought to herself. "The tar wasn't hot enough to cause even the slightest burn, and they used flight feathers instead of down, which are actually quite easy to remove. I can feel my serotonin surging with each feather I deplume."

"Need a hand there?" The words came from Flynn Crowe. Flynn had been on Queenston's campus that day taping one of the ongoing segments of his show, "Alter My Understanding," in which he would set up a table and challenge college students to alter his understanding of issues that were common sense a generation before, but which were now, in the post-rational era, hotly contested. Today, ironically and unfortunately enough, Crowe's challenge had been: "Each fruit is its own distinct category. Alter my understanding." Not surprisingly he, too, was covered in tar and feathers. "You pluck my back, I'll pluck yours."

And there was born a lasting friendship.

Flynn hosted the former professor on *The Cocky Crowe Show* to talk about her ouster from Queenston. This earned him his third and final strike for violating EgoTube's vague policy regarding "promoting hate speech pertaining to fruit."

Flynn's popular EgoTube show and Jordache's academic career now kaput, the two met over a game of craps in Atlantic City to discuss their future.

"We gotta get out of here, Jordache. The coasts are too far gone. I say we posse up and find a good place to start over."

"Are you serious?"

"Dead serious."

"Well then, cheers to that," said Jordache, raising her Mindbender.

Flynn clinked his bourbon into Jordache's glass and both took their sips while the shooter launched a pair of dice across the table. The shooter cut quite an image in his ten-gallon hat, blue jeans, and plaid shirt with snaps.

Double fours. The crowd at the table erupted as the gambling cowboy maintained his streak.

"Where you from, shooter?" shouted Jordache.

"Dallas," he replied without lifting his eyes from the table, where he watched his chips get multiplied by the dealer.

Jordache's eyebrows lifted as she pulled up a map of the US on her phone. "If we want to get away from here, but stay the hell away from LA, too, look at this." She held her phone so Flynn could see her finger on the map. "That's about as far away from both as you can get while staying in the country."

"Dallas, Texas?"

"Dallas, Texas."

"It's hot there."

"It's muggy here. Not to mention we'll probably literally get mugged when we leave the casino."

"That is true."

Another roll. A pair of threes. Big payouts.

"You could get a cowboy hat, ay?" said Jordache.

"And spurs?" Flynn played along.

"Well, sure. You probably want to have a horse in that case, or you might come off as pretentious, you know."

"I think they give you a horse when you get to town," Flynn said in a solid John Wayne voice, but then his face

43

dropped along with his impression. "I don't know about Dallas, Jordache."

"Let fate pick the town. Then we stand up straight, pull our shoulders back, and do the work it takes to at least slow down the collapse of this civilization that's currently on a trajectory aimed straight for bloody hell."

The shooter hit snake eyes.

"I say," said Jordache, "if the shooter stays alive on this next roll, it's Dallas, Texas or bust. If he craps out, we keep looking."

Flynn took a nip of his bourbon and squinted at Jordache. His eyes followed the waves of her long, brown hair. He liked the way the seedy casino lights bounced off her smooth skin and how the velvet of the table brought out the fire in her green eyes. He felt a warmth flush through his body. Some of that warmth was the bourbon coursing through his veins, but still. "Flip that wager, and it's a deal."

"So, he craps out on this roll, we go to Dallas?"

"Yep."

They shook hands.

Flynn had put his time in at the craps table over the years, so he knew he had just swung the odds heavily in favor of a town other than Dallas. "But this shooter ain't going anywhere. The streak is strong in this one. Maybe we can look into Montana or Idaho ..." he began mumbling a series of other possible cities and states, confident in the gamble he was making.

Jordache's intuition throbbed. She dropped a hundred-dollar chip on the Any Seven bet as she imagined the scenery she would soon be seeing in her new Texas town—though it was actually just memories of the opening of the TV show *Dallas* she had watched as a kid, complete with its dated disco theme music.

A different dealer walked up and tapped the current dealer on the shoulder. The casino had enough of this shooter's draining of the house bank. No better way to shake up the mojo of a hot table than to swap out the dealer and dice.

Flynn's cocky grin left his face, and he pulled his bets off the table. "Well, you win," he said.

"What do you mean?" said Jordache. "He hasn't even rolled yet."

The dice launched from the shooter's hand.

"You better work on your drawl, y'all," Flynn said to her. The dice banked off the back wall and tumbled to a stop. "Three plus four equals seven equals craps equals you and me are going to Texas."

Jordache scooped up her four-hundred dollar win from the table and lifted her face toward Flynn with that *come hither* look in her eyes—a look she had never given him before.

Flynn's mind raced in a million directions at once—his canceled show, his impending move to Dallas, which a few minutes ago wasn't even in his world of possibilities, his desire to go on an adventure with this woman—and this freed his passion to take control of the wheel. He put his hands on the sides of Jordache's face and planted a smacker right on the lips.

"Ooh," Jorache said with a giggle, using her hand to fan her face. "You know, back at Queenston, you do that without a consent form signed and notarized in triplicate, and they'd throw you in jail."

"Well, Toto, we ain't in Queenston anymore. Won't even be in Jersey for long, neither," he said, resuming his John Wayne impression. "Dallas, here we come."

The road trip out of Jersey and into Texas gave the two lovebirds twenty-one hours to talk and dream and plot. Their future took shape as miles of concrete and asphalt passed beneath the tires of Flynn's Bronco. Given people's shrinking attention spans, they decided they could make the greatest cultural impact by creating content for Fluttyr Quix, which featured brief video clips. With Jordache's psychological insights and Flynn's biting humor, the two would put out short skits crafted to wake people from the state-crafted stupor in which they found themselves.

They wasted no time at all when they arrived in Dallas. Got hitched and started their own production company, Lobster Flex. Their first release, a three-minute story about restoring romance to life via sacrificial service for others, called "11 Rules for Love + 1," went viral.

Their next Quix flit, "One Order of Chaos, Please: A Baker's Dozen More Rules for Love," would turn out to be one of Fluttyr's most re-flitted flits.

Flynn didn't have spurs yet—it turned out Dallas didn't give you a horse when you arrived in town. But he did don his gambler cowboy hat with a swagger. He and his bride were speaking truth and kickin' up some dust.

Alright. You're all caught up. Back to the grassy knoll . . .

"So?" said Flynn.

"So what?" said Jordache.

"So, what are the three things you think the race-baiters are going to do now?"

"Right, right. One, divide and conquer. They're a contemptible bunch but give the devil his due—they're expert at division. That's how they got where they are. Won't be race anymore, but the methods will be the same. They are a one-trick, sick pony, man. You can rest assured of that. Two, they will continue to attack those who are a threat to their power." Jordache scraped the bottom of the can with a wooden spoon to get another bite of plain tuna in water. "And three—"

A head popped up above the edge of Flynn and Jordache's knoll. Then shoulders. Then a whole man, dressed like a mix between Jimi Hendrix and Jack Sparrow.

"I'm Klaven. With an 'e.' There is one 'e' in Klaven."

Flynn's eyebrows raised. "O . . . kay?"

Klaven lifted a tumbler to his mouth and took what was apparently quite a satisfying sip from the vessel.

Jordache sized up the unusual character, his clothes, and accent. "You're Romani?"

"Let's cut the PC crap. I'm a Gypsy."

"Fair enough," Jordache said.

Klaven extended the vessel to Jordache. "A sip? It's quite salty," he added as if that would encourage Jordache to accept the offer. "I'm a bit of a maven of fine beverages. This one tastes like sorrow."

"Oh, no thank you," Jordache said, lifting her tuna can as if in a toast. "Plenty of salt . . . and sorrow in here."

Flynn put his hands up in a preemptive declination of the tumbler, should he be offered a sip next.

"Suit yourselves," said Klaven. Another swig from his drink and a happy sigh. "Ángel appeared to me in my homeland."

"In Romania?"

"No," said the Gypsy. "Plano. I live in Plano, Texas. Got a little trailer there. This Ángel has sent me on some extensive and time-consuming missions in the past. Thankfully, this one was only about a half-hour drive."

"Oh," said Flynn, giving Jordache a queer look.

"So," Jordache said, "a divine being . . . contacted you?"

"Divine being?" said Klaven with a laugh. "Ángel, my buddy I met in the joint. I got out last week. He's still doin' time. Told me to go to the grassy knolls and find two righteous souls. I love it when he rhymes. Best freestyler in Cell Block 4."

"We'll be sure to let you know if we see any righteous souls," Flynn said, throwing a smirk to Jordache.

"I mean, I'm pretty good, but this guy," she said, pointing at Flynn, "a little more than rough around the edges, if you know what I mean."

"Oh, I can see that," said Klaven, eliciting a *humph* from Flynn. "But, to be exact, he said, 'righteous *enough* souls,' and you are the two."

"And what makes you think that? Just because we're sitting on a grassy knoll? People come here all the time."

"Ángel said to look for the sign of the fish."

"Oh," said Jordache, lifting the tuna can in her hand.

"So, listen close. Ángel said he had a vision. And in that vision, he saw a snake. And the snake hissed in a cycling recitation, 'Beware the Ides of April.'"

"Are you sure it wasn't 'Beware the Ides of March'?" said Flynn. "Sounds like a reference to Julius Caesar."

"No, he was clear. April."

"Ides refers to the day on which debts are due," said Jordache, drawing her eyes into a squint as her mind raced through dozens of possible meanings for the cryptic message.

Flynn looked up. "Tax day?"

"Could be," said Jordache.

"And then . . ."

Jordache and Flynn leaned in toward their odd visitor.

"Time was up for visiting hour. The phone behind the bulletproof glass shut off. And they took Ángel back to his cell."

"He didn't say anything else?" asked Jordache.

"No, he didn't say anything else."

"Oh," she said, disappointed now that Klaven had piqued her interest with his mysterious message.

Klaven's face took on an impish grin. "But you didn't ask if that was all he communicated," he said with a sing-songy delivery. 'Be precise in your wording.' Isn't that advice you give in one of your Quix, Dr. De la Roca?"

49

"Well, yes it is. Touché. I didn't realize you know our work."

"Oh, I know. I follow Lobster Flex on Fluttyr. Never miss a Jordache De La Roca and Flyin' Crowe post."

"That's Flynn," said Flynn, correcting Klaven's mispronunciation of his name.

"Are you sure? Flyin' Crowe sounds better . . . you know, crows fly and all that."

"Yeah, I get it. It's Flynn."

"So, let me be precise in my wording," said Jordache. "Did Ángel communicate anything else to you?"

"As he left, he yanked his arm away from the guard, and he made a circle with his hand, which he then began slowly rotating. Had a horrified look on his face. Then the guard pulled him through the door. And that was it."

Jordache's face looked perplexed. "There's nothing else you can share with us?"

"There is one more thing," said Klaven.

"Yes?" said Jordache.

"You can save fifteen percent on Jeremy's Tasers if you enter promo code GYPSY at checkout."

And with that, he turned on his booted heels and walked off, up and over the small hill, disappearing beyond the horizon of the grassy knoll.

6

Pork & Beans

President Hyden steadied his six-pound bowling ball atop the toddler ramp as he made aim for the ten pins at the end of the lane. Behind him stood Raven DiCherubino, who held zer forehead in zer hand.

Hyden called the meeting at the command of DiCherubino, and as zhe dictated, Abe Z'Bendy, B.S., and Panderson Blasé were there as well. The eunuch and the man sat by the ball return eating bowls of whipped cream-topped gelatin Hyden ordered from the White House kitchen. All four wore custom bowling shirts Hyden had made for them: red with a flaming lightning bolt down the front left, and the words "Hyden Pinz" embroidered on the back.

Blyx was there, too. He didn't need to be, as the humans gathered had such high levels of corruption inherent in their character that they really needed no direct urging from him, but it was his night off, and there was nothing more entertaining than watching these four tools unintentionally conspiring according to Blyx's plan.

Hyden insisted they meet at the bowling lane, installed in the basement of the White House by President Nixon in 1973, because it "has good vibes," as the President put it. He didn't add that it was the one place his wife wouldn't follow him. Gretchen Hyden, Esquire—she was not a lawyer, but after watching every episode of *LA Law* in an epic marathon binge, she inexplicably started appending the title to her name. She was always on Hyden. Grabbing his arm to direct him when he wandered around public events without a clue as to what he should be doing. Telling him just to read the "speechy words," as he referred to them, and not the directions on the teleprompter. Super annoying. But she hated bowling, so Hyden was safe in his Presidential alley.

Hyden released the ball from his trembling fingers and watched with glee as it rolled down the ramp, onto the wooden lane, off the left bumper, off the right bumper, the left bumper again, then slowing to a near stop as it bumped the left corner pin. The pin wobbled for a moment and then tipped over.

"Good job, Mr. President," said DiCherubino, through zer teeth.

"Is it a strike?" asked Hayden in his confused, breathy voice.

"Uh, yes, that's exactly what it is," said DiCherubino, "another strike." It was Hayden's first pin of the night. "Maybe ze should get down to business," zhe said as zhe led the President by the shoulders back to zeir chairs.

"Reminds me of the time I won the Boys Town Bowling Championship," said Hyden. "'Head Pin

Hyden' they called me. Yeah, that's the ticket. Wore a blindfold and bowled barefoot so's I could feel the grain of the wood under my toes. True story, man. No, I'm serious. True story, man. No, I'm serious—"

"Yes, Mr. President," DiCherubino said. "Right this way, Head Pin Hyden."

Hyden reached up. He gently pinched and rubbed DiCherubino's earlobe between his thumb and forefinger while he whispered "pork and beans" to zer. Zhe was used to this particular creepy action by this point, though he usually reserved the bizarre invasion of personal space, and equally bizarre choice of words to whisper, to teen and preteen girls at public events.

DiCherubino sat Hyden down in a chair and placed an afghan over his lap.

"This will not do," DiCherubino said as zhe took command of the meeting.

"Well, maybe ze can get him some bowling lessons," said Panderson Blasé.

"No, you idiot," said DiCherubino. "Not his bowling."

"Head Pin Hyden," the President said with a glazed look in his eye.

"Zhe's talking about the Yucky Race Erasure catastrophe," said Z'Bendy.

"Oh, right," said Blasé, who was hired by SNN more for his tailored silver suit and quirky eyeglass frame—and his willingness to promote any message powerful elites demanded of him—than his intellect.

DiCherubino continued. "Panderson, have you made any headway tracking the source of the Yucky Race Erasure?"

"My bosses in the FBI and CIA . . . I mean, my sources have tracked some odd activity near Davos in Switzerland."

DiCherubino's and Z'Bendy's postures stiffened at the word Davos.

"It's not *them*," said Blasé. "Those are zour guys . . . Well, ze're their guys, but πü≈ know what I mean."

"Whoever it is, zour plan to divide, conquer, and control is falling apart now," said DiCherubino. "Not to mention, zour Colorful People Count logo doesn't even make sense anymore." Zhe slammed a report down on the table. "These are zour latest poll numbers. Because of the Yucky Race Erasure, the Progressocrat Party shrinks by the day. Racial smears—just like that, gone as a tactic to scare and anger people to our side."

"Enough talk about race," Z'Bendy said. "That's over. Ze need to use other tactics to consolidate—"

DiCherubino had hatred in zer eyes as zhe interrupted Z'Bendy. "Xi'm well aware of that. Don't mansplain the obvious to xe."

"How many times do I have to tell πü≈," whined Z'Bendy, adding DiCherubino's obligatory second person pronoun gagging sound, "I'm not a man. I had my member removed years ago. Gender and maleness and manhood are not related to biology, so removing part of my biology is a clear indicator that I'm not a man. It makes perfect—"

"Pretzel logic, I know," DiCherubino said, cutting him off.

Blasé flicked a piece of lint from the sharkskin sport coat he wore over his gaudy Hyden Pinz bowling shirt. "I thought πü≈," he gagged, "called this meeting to talk about equity."

DiCherubino's face took on a sudden calmness. "Xi did." Zhe took a moment to stare into each of the men's faces, well, men's and former man's faces. "Ze all know equity is an unachievable 'goal,' which is the whole reason it is going to be zour new focus. That said, opportunities to rise for all people abound. Ze can't have that. It's time to get rid of cash and require all deeds—for real estate, cars, whatever—to be digital. Ze can't manipulate cash, but once ze put every penny on the grid, ze'll control the board like ze're playing chess against a bunch of shaved, blind monkeys."

"I think I get why the monkeys in zour scenario are shaved, but the word 'blind' is offensive," Z'Bendy said with no confidence in his delivery.

"Oh, grow up," DiCherubino snapped.

Z'Bendy folded his arms in a pout.

"The point is," DiCherubino continued, "once all wealth is digitized, ze can leverage access to money to ban any speech and behavior ze don't like. And ultimately, ze can keep poor people poor, rich people beholden to zux, and crush the middle class as ze force moral insanity and conformity upon them, thus increasing equity."

The space between Blasé's plucked eyebrows tried to scrunch, but the Botox from his injection earlier that day left them at perfectly unnatural ease. "That doesn't make sense. That would mean greater inequity, right?"

DiCherubino answered him with an evil grin. "It's time to go digital. In the meantime, keep looking for the culprits responsible for the Yucky Race Erasure. If ze find them, maybe ze can force them to undo the Pandora's box of racial unity they've unleashed on the world, which from an antiracist perspective was a racist thing to do."

"Will do," said Blasé. "There's definitely someone on the inside with access to the 'loss of function' research zour guys were working on to learn how to erase racial differences to make sure no one ever did erase racial differences. And if anyone were to figure out how to erase racial differences, then ze would eventually have the technology to recreate racial differences. But zour labs haven't put all the pieces together yet. The best they can do is shift people's skin tone darker or lighter. Same with facial features and hair—they can cause modifications all in one direction or another—which would just keep people indivisible by race."

"Well, that does zux no good," said DiCherubino.

"Also," continued Blasé, "even the alterations our guys can make—they only know how to achieve those in a lab setting. Whoever discovered how to transmit those changes to all humans at the same time—well, they're clearly brilliant."

Blyx roared in laughter as he dimension-skipped to a hot tub in Putz, Switzerland, where he had gathered Blaze Eppy, OAC, and Michelangelo von Cappuccino.

"This tastes like bubbles," OAC said as she held her glass of kombucha above the water of the hot tub.

"Bubbles don't have a flavor. The flavor is from fermented tea—" Von Cappuccino started explaining before being interrupted by Eppy.

"Some powerful people are not happy with us. I mean, they don't know who we are—but they figured out that The Great Race Blender wasn't some kind of cosmic accident."

OAC's eyes opened wide. "You mean the right wingnuts? They just can't let go of their racism!" She slammed her fist down, splashing water into her eyes.

"No, they're fine with one race. It's the Left. The elites. Our people. One of my contacts in the CIA used the word 'heartbroken' to describe the Hyden Administration."

"But I saw them on TV," said Von Cappuccino. "I mean, Hyden had the White House lit up in beige. He said he was excited that there was a single race so he could now focus on attacking sexism and transphobia because straight cis men make all things bad."

"I know, I know," said Eppy. "That's what he said in public, but behind the scenes, his handlers were fuming. They said 'racist' was their favorite label to apply to their political opponents, so having only one race of humans took the joy out of politics."

OAC held her arm up and admired it glistening in hot tub water and moonlight. "Well, I don't regret it at all. I love the new color of my skin. It goes so well with my evening attire."

Von Cappuccino squirted water into the air like a mini fountain by squeezing his hand into a fist over and over. "I kind of miss having different races. In interviews, I used to say that humanity's greatest problems are *whiteness* and *white supremacy* and *white privilege.* That really made me feel good about myself. I don't know what to say in interviews now. It's so confusing."

Eppy moved Von Cappuccino's tam tassel out of his face and patted his shoulder. "I know, I know. But we have a new battle to wage."

"You mean, like how some people still don't state their pronouns in their social media bios, which is an act of first-degree murder against trans people?" said OAC.

"We'll get to that," Eppy said, "but there's something else that's brewing."

Von Cappuccino stopped making a fountain with his hand. "What is it?"

"*Envision no belongings,*" Eppy sang as a wily smile overtook his face.

Blyx beamed, for he was already several steps ahead of his hot tub-stewed stooges.

7

Digitize Your Life

Judy Ravioli dipped a blood-red strawberry into melted chocolate and took a bite. She sat on the sun deck of Paradies Café. The eatery lived up to its name. It was perched at the base of a hanging valley that overlooked a mountain view and the flowing water of a blue river below. But Judy was not there for sensual pleasure. She was on a mission for Ace MacDonald.

Ravioli leaned back, struggling to keep the traditional Swiss dirndl she wore as a disguise in place. She brushed her wig's golden Swiss-maiden braids aside and squinted her eyes as she listened in on the conversation taking place at the table behind her.

Trapper Hyden had many vices, but everyone knew number one on his list was fondue. Being the child of a wealthy elite, only the best fondue would do for Trapper, which meant that Ravioli had to travel to St. Moritz, Switzerland to spy on him for her boss.

"Let us get out of this place," said the blonde woman sitting across from Trapper. Her voice had an odd, gravelly falsetto quality to it with a vaguely South African-sounding accent.

"But we haven't even sampled the Beaufort yet," Trapper said, sounding as if he might cry should he be forced to skip the next course.

Ravioli motioned to a waiter as if she was drinking from an imaginary glass. She attempted to say, but did not achieve, a German phrase she read from the translator on her phone. "Kann . . . ich . . . bitte . . . Ihre . . . Weinkarte . . . sehen?" Her voice had an oddly appealing gopher-like articulation to it.

The waiter handed Ravioli a rather large, leather menu. "Of course. Here is our wine list. I speak English, Frau," he said with an irritated look on his face.

"Perfect," said Ravioli to herself, smiling in approval at the height of the menu. As the waiter walked off, Ravioli attached a tiny camera to the top of the wine list, then eased it up to capture the action behind her.

"I do not think I should give it to you here. You never know who might be watching," the blonde woman said.

"The Big Cheese insists I carry out all the deals in public places. Says it makes for better plausible deniability should anyone get the wrong . . . well, the right idea."

The woman rolled her eyes and reached down to the oversized purse at her side. She lifted out a spherical object covered by a scarf.

Ravioli couldn't believe what she was hearing. She dared not turn around, but she looked up to make sure her camera was capturing all of this.

"Take it off," said Trapper, who was only half paying attention as he wiped some Gruyère off his chin with a napkin.

"Before I do, the deal is clear?" his dinner guest said.

"Yeah, yeah," said Trapper. "I take this one tonight. Your boss gets a phone call from The Big Cheese. Then, we meet up at—"

The blonde woman reached out and touched Trapper's hand. "*Shh.*"

"Right," said Trapper. He raised a small book from his lap to his chest and opened it facing her. "We meet up at here . . ." he stopped speaking as he pointed at a section in the book, "and here . . ." again pointing at his book, "and just like that, we'll all be *Bowling at the White House,*" he said with a wink.

She lifted the scarf.

Trapper grabbed the snow globe quickly, not to hide it, but to make room for the Beaufort, which was being dropped off at the table. He placed the bribe on his coat next to him and wasted no time at all cooking his next hit of gourmet cheese.

Back in her room at Château Manigances, Ravioli swapped out her dirndl for some sweats and tossed her Swiss-maiden wig onto the floor.

Her face lit up in the screen of a laptop as she viewed the video she shot at Paradies Café. Rewinding, watching again, in slow-motion and reverse. She put on her headphones. The audio captured Trapper basically admitting that the snow globe was a bribe for access to the

"Big Cheese" and connecting the whole deal to the White House.

Eesh, Ravioli thought to herself as the camera caught the unusually muscular arms and shoulders of the woman sitting across from Trapper. Something about the woman's eyes looked familiar, but Ravioli couldn't remember where she had seen her before.

She watched the two seconds of video that revealed the snow globe over and over looking for clues. She could make out something yellow. It looked like it might be a submarine of some sort. But the focal point of the globe was obscured by cheese dripping from a cracker in Trapper's hand.

Trapper's enthusiasm for melted cheese made him careless. After he and the blonde left the restaurant, Ravioli found the small book Trapper had been pointing to on his seat. It was Trapper's second greatest vice, CrazyLibs, the book in which you fill in the blanks with parts of speech to concoct hilarious "ad-lib" stories.

Ravioli cracked open Trapper's CrazyLibs "Fun in Europe" Edition and began reading. No skills of deep analysis or deduction were needed. Instead of clever entries, Trapper wrote in what he thought were the "correct answers" for each blank. He inherited his intellect from his father. Fortunately for Ravioli, he also wrote his itinerary in the margins of the book. Next stop: Zimbabwe, Africa.

•   •   •

Jordache de la Roca was deep in sleep during a midday nap. Her mind a movie screen of dreams, she watched the last clip from her and Flynn's Quix video, *One Order of Chaos, Please: A Baker's Dozen More Rules for Love.* The skit was a dramatization of a post-apocalyptic love story, the inverse of the Garden of Eden: Adam and Eve, instead of being the first two humans on Earth were the last two. Jordache knew the scene she should see, that of Eve giving Adam a copy of Carl Jung's *Modern Man in Search of a Soul,* which he then throws into a blazing fire. Instead, in her dream, Adam gives Eve a tulip. Eve extends her arm, as if ready to toss the flower into the fire, when Adam grabs her wrist and pulls it to his chest. Jordache watched the scene in a loop. She could not see Clive, an angel, sitting at the film projector in her mind, but there he was, reloading the reel over and over again.

She woke up and called Flynn, who was working on a Quix at their Lobster Flex studio. "Meet me at the knoll."

•   •   •

Flynn looked around Dealey Plaza from the grassy knoll. He could see the famous Texas School Book Depository beyond some trees, a white "X" painted on the street where President Kennedy was shot in 1963. Then he watched Jordache walk toward him at a quick clip up Elm Street.

They sat on the steps on the upward slope of the knoll, and Jordache shared her dream with Flynn.

"A tulip, huh?"

"Yes, a tulip," she said. Jordache took a long pause and chose her words carefully. "There is a great darkness upon us. And we must send a message of life out from the Father of lights."

"That is from your dream?"

"Yes."

"What is the message? How do we send it?" asked Flynn.

Jordache's eyes scanned left to right along the plaza. "I was hoping we could find out here. I know it's unlikely, but I'm thinking that odd man we met here last time can help us."

"Klaven? The Gypsy?"

"Exactly." Jordache reached into her purse and pulled out a can of tuna.

"I don't think that's—"

"The sign of the fish." The voice came from behind them. It was Klaven. "Thought I was gonna have to wait here all day for you two."

"How did you know we'd be here?" said Flynn.

"How does one know anything?" Klaven nodded his head slowly as if to highlight the profundity of his words. His face cracked into a smile. "Ángel told me you'd be here."

Jordache spoke. "So, how are we going to use—"

She and Klaven said "tulips" at the same time.

"Jinx, you owe me a Coke," said Klaven.

Jordache let out an awkward chuckle.

"No, I'm serious," he said, motioning to a nearby street vendor. "I'm thirsty, and I don't have any cash."

"I'll get you a soda," Jordache said as the three started walking toward the vendor. "So, how do tulips play into this?"

"Very simple. Ángel said the one with the sign of the fish and her husband are to withdraw all their money in cash and convert it into—"

"Bitcoin!" said Flynn.

The vendor handed Klaven a bottle of soda. "I don't take Bitcoin."

Klaven shook his head, no.

Jordache handed money to the vendor, and the three began walking back toward the grassy knoll.

"Doge?" said Flynn.

"No," said Klaven. "That would be crazy. Ángel said you are to use it to buy tulips."

"Ah, now that makes *complete* sense," said Flynn, shaking his head.

"Tulip bulbs to be exact."

Jordache was unusually quiet, her face still.

"Let me get this straight," said Flynn. "Jordache and I are going to take out all of our money and buy tulip bulbs with it? Because a guy in prison said we should?"

"Yes, that is exactly what you are going to do. Well, take all cash out, yes, spend half on tulip bulbs. Hold onto the rest for expenses and further instructions."

"Not so sure that's better. And are you pouring your life savings into tulip bulbs, too?"

"Of course not," said Klaven with a chuckle. "I told you, I'm a Gypsy. I have no savings."

"That's a negative stereotype," said Jordache.

"Indeed it is. But that doesn't change the fact that I'm broke. Followed some really bad financial advice from Ángel last year that wiped me out."

Flynn turned to walk away. "Let's get out of here, Jordache."

Jordache grabbed Flynn's hand. "I know this sounds crazy, Flynn, but I think we should do what he says. I know it's asking a lot, and it's a leap of faith. But, somehow . . . our visions are lining up. I mean, think about how our lives have gone the last few months. We lost our careers only to find success on Fluttyr, in part, because some guy in a casino rolled a seven. I get that this is crazy, but our whole life is crazy."

Flynn looked at Jordache long and hard. Her lush hair, skin shining under a smoggy Dallas sky, eyes challenging the green of the unkempt shrubs behind her—he didn't have a chance. He turned to Klaven. "And what are we going to do with these tulip bulbs? Hold them as some sort of investment, like the Dutch tulip bubble from way back when?"

"You know your history. Good. But, no. There is only one thing to do with tons of tulip bulbs."

"And what's that?"

"We plant them."

"For when spring comes," Jordache said, "this will be the message from the . . ."

"Father of lights," all three said in unison, though Flynn's tone implied the words as a question.

"Exactly," said Klaven.

Flynn gave him a hard stare. "We'll need to sleep on this."

"No time," said Klaven. "Ángel had quite a bit to say today. President Hyden is making a big announcement tonight. It's not good."

•   •   •

Flynn pulled the used box truck he and Jordache had just purchased for cash onto a dirt road leading into Gopherwood Farm. Klaven sat between them in the middle of the bench seat. He whistled the theme from *Green Acres* between his teeth, to Flynn's chagrin, as they made their way to the center of the vast property.

"I love these rural areas," Flynn said as he got out of the truck. "Off the grid . . ." He took in a deep breath of fresh country air and smiled at the bucolic setting while Klaven knocked on the large door of an enormous red barn. "It's like taking a step back in time, away from all the trappings of civilization."

The doors opened automatically and revealed what looked like a huge sports bar inside. Flynn sighed and his shoulders dropped at the sight of the technology.

There were screens everywhere, large and small, with sporting events and news channels tuned in from around the world. Above the bar was a movie theater-sized screen displaying a single mother of three wrestling a monkey for rent money—the latest contestants on a new gladiator-style game show promoted by the Hyden Administration called *What Have You Got to Lose?* There was a

Smokey and the Bandit pinball machine against the wall. A dartboard. A mechanical bull in the corner.

A bartender dried a glass as he chatted with the sole patron who sipped a beer at the bar.

It was such a sight to take in, they didn't even notice the overall-wearing man standing in the middle of it all.

"Welcome to the Too Soon Saloon. Can I help you?"

"What's . . . what's this all about?" said Flynn, his eyes locked on the gladiator game as the mother gave the monkey a solid backhand.

"Well, that's depravity," the man said, pointing at the main screen. "Helps keep me motivated."

"Motivated to commit depravity?" said Flynn.

The man smiled. "Quite the opposite. Noah. The name's Noah," he said extending his hand.

The three introduced themselves.

Jordache removed the can of tuna from her purse and held it so Noah could see it.

"The sign of the fish," said Noah, nodding his head a few times. "Tulip bulbs are out this way."

"A dream?" said Flynn.

"Yes, a dream," answered the farmer.

Though the four had help from Noah's farmhands, they were still covered in sweat and dirt after loading the truck with tulip bulbs.

As they brushed the dust off their clothes back at the Too Soon Saloon, Klaven nodded toward one of the screens on the wall. Hyden approached the podium in the White House Press Room.

Noah clicked an app on his phone, and the audio from that screen filled the room.

"I've called this press conference today for an important announcement," said Hyden. He hugged a folder. Everyone assumed it held his notes, but it actually contained his childhood copy of *The Little Engine That Could*.

He leaned into the microphone. "By executive order, I am bashing cabbage."

Hyden's press secretary—a pansexual, throuple member, little person, furry of Asian, African, Aboriginal, and South American descent named Alouette Jean-Luc le Pew—ascended a stepladder and whispered in the President's ear.

Hyden looked back into the camera. "This little whippersnapper here says I'm not bashing cabbage. I'm banning cash. But, I say, why can't we do both? Walk and chew gum, man. Do it all the time. The one thing I know is . . ." he leaned in and spoke in an odd whispery voice, "We are about to make your life so much better because . . ." and then he awkwardly raised his voice to a shout, "we'll know where you spend every cent of your money!"

Z'Bendy emerged from stage right of the Press Room and led the President away from the podium. Reporters shouted questions, but Hyden just looked over his shoulder and said, "It's sherbet time, so that's all folks. The dwarf'll take it from here."

Le Pew grabbed the mic. "Americans, you have twenty-four hours to turn your cash into your bank, which will then be digitized and available for your use immediately via your ATM cards, online checking, and approved smartphone apps. After that, your cash will be worthless."

"He's taking our money?" shouted a reporter. "Why is the President doing this?"

"Look. If you want your money, you can keep your money. You just need to digitize it. The President is doing this to make the lives of Americans better by making it possible for us to trace every transaction you make via a new collaboration between banks and the federal government," said the diminutive furry. "Lacking privacy in purchasing will make it easier for Americans to spend their money in ways that the President approves of, which makes you freer. Any other questions?"

"What about gold?" another reporter yelled.

"Glad you mentioned that. You gotta turn in all your gold, too. The US government will give you current market value for your gold if you turn it in freely. If you don't, it will be confiscated and not reimbursed."

"What about cryptocurrency?"

"We already control cryptocurrency, so you can keep that."

"You do?"

"Satoshi Nakamoto?" she chuckled. "Try CIA." Le Pew scanned the room as the reporters burst into applause, since the press and the Progressocrat Party they covered were one and the same.

Noah turned down the volume on the TV.

Jordache pointed to the briefcase filled with cash—the one that she and Flynn brought—sitting on Noah's desk. "Are you turning that in to the bank?"

"Heck no," said Noah. "I've got a connection in town. I'll be trading that cash today for a collection of Pökermang cards. I suggest you do the same with whatever cash you've got left over."

"Those are the further instructions for your cash I told you about," said Klaven with a pleased smile.

"Pökermang, the Scandinavian-Cuban kid's card game?" said Flynn.

"Kid's game, yes," said Noah. "But also, this will be the currency of the new underground."

"You learned about this in a dream?"

Noah winked as he brought down the lid of the briefcase and snapped it shut.

8

Poof

The US descended into mayhem. Phone lines and internet cables practically glowed from an explosion of activity as those who had large amounts of cash and gold scrambled to find alternatives to the executive order.

After these citizens realized this was an international mandate coordinated by the Hyden Administration and the UN, they gave up, traded their cash in, and got back to scrolling through their selfies and other inappropriate images on their phones.

Jordache, Flynn, and Klaven wasted no time in their horticultural endeavor. They decided it would be best to work late at night, as their activity was certainly unusual. From midnight until dawn, they planted tulip bulbs, starting at Dealey Plaza and working their way outward anywhere they could find soil. In flower beds, in undeveloped lots, in dirt patches and below the grass on public lawns. They planted ... and planted ... and planted. The same day two. And day three. Wherever there was soil, they planted bulbs.

Back to Noah for another load of tulip bulbs. And back to the perimeter of the Dallas landmark to dig and plant.

Flynn wiped his soiled brow with his denim shirt sleeve. "I know you've had these dreams, but these bulbs aren't even going to blossom for months. Why the urgency?"

"If you plant them, they will come," said Jordache.

"*Field of Dreams*?"

"More like field of Jungian dreams. Carl Jung said dreams are often 'the richest jewel in the treasure-house of psychic experience.'"

"Translation please."

"If we don't plant the bulbs in winter, they won't be here to blossom in spring."

Flynn nodded his head. "Hopefully, this all produces more than some weird baseball player ghosts. Speaking of weird things, where's Klaven? I thought he was gonna be in the trenches with us."

At that moment, Flynn and Jordache watched as nine figures appeared in the fog and slowly approached them.

"And here are the baseball player ghosts," said Flynn.

The phantoms turned out to be people. "It's me, Klaven. Sorry I'm late, but I brought friends. Ángel and a couple of his buddies just got out of the joint. Told them we could use some help."

Ángel stepped out from the others. He was dressed in all white. White slacks. White dress shirt. White slip-on loafers with no socks. Shaved head.

"You're going to help us?" said Jordache.

"We heard you have Pökermang cards."

"Yeah. I might have some Pökermang cards."

Without looking, Ángel made a sound with his mouth, like one would make to direct a trained dog, and his subordinates moved quickly toward the truck and grabbed armfuls of tulip bulbs.

He moved his head toward some untouched soil; his crew sprang into action and began digging holes for the bulbs.

"Aren't you gonna help?" asked Flynn.

"I don't like getting my hands dirty," said Ángel. "My love language is encouragement."

Jordache and Flynn asked him about the Ides of April warning he had communicated via Klaven.

"I receive the prophecy, reality provides the interpretation," he told them.

"That's . . . a . . . very helpful, Ángel," said Flynn as he walked back to his most recently dug hole and dropped a bulb inside with attitude.

•   •   •

"The foundation has been laid, Panderson. A clay base today. But very soon, this pedestal will display the largest golden structure ever built. Reporting live from Gaslight Island . . ."

The SNN reporter stood in front of the clay base she described. Off to the side were the head and torch of the Statue of Liberty, which were being unceremoniously carted off to be discarded. Hyden had renamed Liberty

Island in New York "Gaslight Island" and was using the gold purchased from Americans to craft a golden calf in honor of his recent banning of eating beef. Well, elites could still eat beef by purchasing "cow-killing offsets," but these were too expensive for the average citizen. The golden calf would be illuminated by a series of gaslight-looking lamps—though the lamps would actually be solar powered because, it was reasoned, twelve small gas-lit lamps would bring about a global flood due to Climate Change™.

The SNN screen broke for a commercial from its sponsor, Gneuter Rx, before returning to Blasé for the next segment of his Big Stories broadcast. "Many predicted improved social relations following the end of racial differences, but ze've seen the opposite. Why?" He pursed his lips as he awaited a response from his guest, Raven DiCherubino.

"Racism was just the tip of an oppressive iceberg whose mass below the surface is actually inequity frozen into place by the heteronormative patriarchy. Losing skin color distinctions just made it harder to see who the bad guys are. You would see a white person before and know, there is a white supremacist who is oppressing non-whites and instituting fascism by their existence—"

One of Blasé's other talking-head guests spoke up, "But, you were white, weren't you?"

"Xi am trans." DiCherubino's glare could melt steel.

"Oh, of course." The talking head was a Republican senator elected to fight the Left, so, naturally, he tapped the white flag pin on his lapel and deferred to DiCherubino.

"And by xy self-selection as trans, Xi am automatically a member of the most marginalized and victimized of all groups into which people like xe categorize people. The fact that the federal government, the military, the FBI, the CIA, academia, Hollywood, and all multi-national corporations promote transgenderism exhaustively is all the proof you need of zour marginalization. But back to xy point. Inequity and the heteronormative patriarchy are evils that have only increased now that racial distinctions are gone. And ze must attack both without mercy. Ze might not be able to see who the white men are anymore, but scratch the surface of any straight cis-gendered man you come across, and you'll find zour true enemy below— a patriarchal fascist festering in his inequity."

At that moment, the screen flashed with a graphic that looked like an election result between two candidates. But instead of political candidates, it had Blasé and DiCherubino—their faces and names—and instead of election vote percentages and party affiliation, it revealed their net worth and "job title":

Panderson Blasé Net Worth: $280 million
Job Title: Propagandist

Raven DiCherubino Net Worth: $315 million
Job Title: Grifter

The visual was disrupted by sporadic, subliminally rapid flashes of a red tulip.

SNN producers scrambled.

"What the hell is going on?" yelled Panderson as he looked at a somewhat accurate estimation of his net worth and a fully accurate job title on his monitor.

DiCherubino ripped the headphone out of zer ear and the mic off of zer shirt and stormed off-screen.

The SNN broadcast had been hacked.

•   •   •

Blasé helped Hyden roll his child-sized bowling ball down the ramp, and both watched excitedly as it bounced back and forth off the gutter guards, slowly making its way toward the pins.

DiCherubino spoke to Z'Bendy, but at an agitated volume so that the President and SNN anchor could hear zer, too. "Ze've got to keep zour eye on the ball, which some of zux are failing to do!"

"C'mon," Blasé said to the President, "I think that last comment was our cue."

"Cue balls in bowling? Ridiculous," Hyden said as he shuffled toward the table. "Won't even knock down a pin. Now ping pong. There's a game, Jack."

DiCherubino let out an exaggerated exhalation of air.

"Mama's mad again," Hyden said as he sat down and watched his bowling ball continue to inch down the lane.

"Ze've been treating the American people as zour enemy. But they're not."

Blasé nodded as if he was listening to a guest on his show. "That's right. They're good people."

"They're not good people," DiCherubino snapped. "They're weak people. They are a conquered people, and ze are their masters. And the most pathetic part is, it wasn't even hard. A little peer pressure from a couple 'experts' regurgitated by the beautiful empty suits on TV, and ze had them."

Blasé glared at DiCherubino as he straightened the lapel of his sharkskin coat.

DiCherubino was right. The Hyden Administration trampled the people's Constitutional rights ever since ol' Moe was sworn in, and not enough Americans objected or did anything at all to draw back its abuse of power. But the real crackdown took place in the aftermath of the SNN hack. The Hyden Administration persecuted those who wrote, spoke, or even memed about it. Blocked from social media. Fired from their jobs. Some were assaulted in the streets by mobs. The easiest way to silence them, though, was to freeze their bank accounts. And unless they had Pökermang cards they could use in the underground, they were out of luck. Most of the remaining dissenters who weren't already "in line" got in line quick.

Z'Bendy smiled. "And now, ze need to focus on bringing the lifestyles of the masses down to a more . . . sustainable level."

"Right. Say, that of a 14th century European peasant," said DiCherubino. "But with lots more dysfunctional sex, abortion, and drugs."

Hyden's eyes opened wide as his bowling ball nudged, but did not knock over, the right corner pin at the end of the alley. "I remember 14th century Europe. My mom would tell me, 'Moey, don't forget your jacket, or you'll catch the Black Death from a rat with a head cold.' True story, man."

Blasé looked at DiCherubino and Z'Bendy. "Ze have people under control now, at their current lifestyle. Ze manipulate . . . I mean *manage* their resources, and a happy population is easy to control. Why return to serfdom?"

"Climate Change™," said DiCherubino and Z'Bendy in unison before bursting into laughter.

Blasé nodded. "Ah. That makes sense."

"The elites can keep their lifestyles by purchasing carbon . . ." Z'Bendy could barely keep from giggling with each word he uttered "offsets . . . because that money they spend magically reduces the carbon their lavish lifestyles . . . produce . . . you finish," he said to DiCherubino.

"And the masses will have no choice but to live in big cities in small apartments with no air conditioning, travel by public transit . . . scratch that . . . by bike. They will eat insect protein cooked on electric stoves—when ze allow them to use electricity, that is." Zhe laughed, tears welling up in zer eyes. "It's so breathtakingly delicious."

"The bug protein is delicious?" said Blasé.

"Ha! Xi wouldn't touch that stuff. Xi eat veal and foie gras."

"I thought you were a vegan?"

"Xi am a vegan once removed. The baby cows and geese eat grass and grain, and Xi eat them. The point is, elites will live as they do now. Ze control the elites, and the virus-like masses live—or not—at zour pleasure."

But there were three hot-tub soakers who had other virus-related plans. Plans coordinated by none other than Blyx, of course.

Blyx had a cadre of programmers under the influence of his pyramid of demons who devised a virus that would equalize all financial accounts around the world—and I mean all financial accounts: checking, savings, investments, business accounts, personal accounts, little kids' college funds, cryptocurrencies, you name it. This was all made possible because of the Hyden Administration's digitization of all money around the world in the first place.

The stooges prepared to send the final implementation code to Anonymous.

"Are you ready?" said Von Cappuccino.

"I want to be the one who does it," said OAC with a little girl pouty face.

"But it's my phone," said Von Cappuccino.

"Oh, let her do it," said Eppy.

OAC's face took on a tart smile as she reached her arm out of the water and pressed a glowing "submit" button on Von Cappuccino's phone. She let out an ecstatic squeal.

And with that one click, OAC equalized the amounts in all financial accounts of the Earth to a fraction of a penny and erased all digital receipts of ownership, including home titles. Like magic. *Poof!*

"Cheers to Darwin," said OAC.

"I think you mean Marx," said Von Cappuccino.

"Oh, right. I always get those two confused."

Eppy raised his glass of kombucha out of the water. "To equity."

"To equity," said OAC and Von Cappuccino, as glasses clinked, and demons howled in glee into the night.

9

Zeke's Wild Safari

President Hyden walked into the White House Press Room and headed toward an open reporter chair. Z'Bendy scurried to his side and redirected him to the podium.

"Remarkable times, yes." Hyden looked down at his hands. "Always wanted to be more tan. Well, butter my backside and call me a biscuit—look at me now! Then, we don't know how, but everyone has almost no money—just like my policies were intended to accomplish, but much quicker."

DiCherubino cough-spoke, "Teleprompter," to get Hyden back on track.

"Right," said Hyden as he squinted at the screen and slowly read the words out loud. "Take question . . . from Press. Call on . . . Jimbo Accosted. He's one of ours."

Jimbo shrunk in his seat and looked at the floor.

Ember, a reporter from SNN spoke up. Normally a Hyden ally, she was not too happy about all the money she earned selling out journalism and her country being dramatically reduced. "Not only have all accounts been equalized, but when people put money into the bank, nothing shows up."

Blyx had been around long enough to know that the innovative, the driven, those who knew how to organize and provide useful goods and services and achieve long-term goals would quickly accumulate wealth again. So, he made sure the virus that his stooges delivered in their banking hack would automatically distribute all new deposits globally to all individual accounts. This disrupted the corrupt from gaming the system for their own benefit as well, and though it hurt Blyx to prevent them from this evil, they had to take one for the team—Blyx had to think of the greater evil.

Hyden stared blankly at the reporter.

"What do you have to say about this, Mr. President?" Ember asked.

Hyden hugged his folder containing *The Little Engine That Could* and whispered, "A penny saved is a penny earned."

Hyden motioned to Alouette Jean-Luc le Pew. She ascended her stepladder. Hyden gave her head a quick sniff. He looked disappointed. "Just not the same as a kid."

Z'Bendy took Hyden by the arm and led him away as the press shouted questions.

Hyden winked in their direction, then looked at his Press Secretary. "Take it away, shorty."

Le Pew spoke into the mic. "Stop spreading fake news about the Equity Miracle. Banking investigators have found that when a deposit is made, it is split approximately eight billion ways, the number of people on earth—so one eight-billionth of the deposit does make it into the individual's account—it's totally fair because equity fairly redistributes money you earn with your labor to other people who did not earn it. Because our current monetary units are rounded to the hundredths place, you do not see the deposit—but it's there. Not only that, but I do want to add, all debt was removed by the virus, and the government will be automatically depositing a monthly 'living wage' of five thousand dollars into all Americans' accounts."

"But that living wage is being split eight billion ways," Ember said, as she started to choke up thinking that she would not even be able to afford her daily oat milk latte at Starbanks. "It won't even reach one cent in our accounts."

"You're forgetting, you'll get a cut of everyone else's living wage, too, which means that every American will now receive approximately . . ." she said as she flipped through the pages in her binder to find the figure, "two-hundred and nine dollars every month."

"That's not a living wage. And won't it just inflate the currency since you're giving the same amount to everyone?"

"What's with her?" said Le Pew, motioning to Ember. "It's like Miss Negative Nancy over here. My advice is that if you want to see those bank balances increase, work harder. The workers have nothing to lose but their chains."

Jimbo slowly sat up in his seat. "Speaking of losing chains, there is a rumor that the President . . ." he looked down at an index card in his hand ". . . is working on a bold new initiative regarding crime?"

"I'm glad you brought that up," said Le Pew. "We all know that the only causes of crime are white supremacy and inequity. Well, with one race and everyone having the same amount of money, I am glad to announce on the President's behalf that crime is over. Today, the President will sign what he calls the 'Pandora's Box' executive order, which will immediately release all federal, state, and local prisoners."

Ember spoke up. "But some prisoners are violent."

Le Pew looked down at her notes. "Prisons are racist."

"But there is only one race now."

"Yes, there is only one race—and that race is not white. That means there are zero white inmates in prison now. If that's not white supremacy, I don't know what is. Plus, we need the prison facilities for youth gender transition clinics . . . so beautiful and caring." Le Pew looked into the camera as she choked up a little. "We've got a lot of kids to mutilate, America. Let's get busy."

Blyx jumped up and clicked his cloven-hoofed heels.

•　•　•

Those with the greatest prior investment in society kept doing what they always did—they worked hard to produce goods and services: those with children, people of faith, business owners, those who enjoyed using their talents, the ambitious, true artists.

But there were just enough people who were not invested to throw the system into chaos. When Equity was forced upon humanity, those who had been only begrudgingly working stopped—the lazy, the resentful, the narcissistic, the nihilistic. They were now automatically getting their *fair* share of the income generated by those who did work as well as their two hundred and nine dollars from the government, after all. And they weren't going to work for more money when it would contribute less than a penny to their own accounts. Their absence in the labor force quickly led to a scarcity of products and services.

The resourceful set up bartering networks for physical goods and services and protection to meet their most basic needs. As Noah predicted, Pökermang cards became the currency of the new underground. They skyrocketed in value from the time Jordache and Flynn traded half of their wealth for a large collection of the cards.

The only real wealth anyone had was their physical property. But with all digital records dissolved, it was up to each property owner to prove to those around him that he was planning on maintaining that ownership by force. Having over four hundred million guns in the country helped some achieve that objective, at least in the US.

Worse yet, EgoTube, in one of the most unfortunate coincidences ever, happened to be showing a *Purge* movie marathon the very day Hyden signed his Pandora's Box executive order. As one might expect, barbarism erupted across the nation as people fought for homes, vehicles, food, and, of course, Pökermang cards.

The only societies that fared well were those which had not discarded their values over the ages. Tribes in Africa, Asia, and South America, religious-based societies in the Middle East, rural communities, including a few in America like the Amish. But the West overall—the secular, industrialized nations—were reduced to a state of mobocracy.

Jordache and Flynn could not protect their home and execute Operation Tulip at the same time. They abandoned their condo to a gang of Antifa members wearing "Love is Love" shirts, and with Klaven in tow, went to Gopherwood Farm.

They had gotten to know Noah after buying truckload after truckload of tulip bulbs. Noah told them they could stay with him if things got rough. The farmer had a loyal crew that maintained his farm. Given that he had food and lodging for his farmhands in exchange for their work—and the fact that he was armed to the teeth—Gopherwood Farm was able to maintain its own security.

"I really appreciate you letting us stay here," said Jordache.

"We have some sleeping bags out in the truck," said Flynn. "We can just take a little corner of your barn once the bar shuts down each night. We'll be out late planting anyway."

Noah chuckled.

"What?" said Flynn.

"Well," Noah said, "you won't need to sleep on the floor. You're gonna sleep below the floor."

Klaven maintained the same grin he always seemed to have on his face, while Jordache and Flynn straightened up with concern.

"Follow me," said Noah.

They approached the mechanical bull. Noah gave its tail three quick tugs, and the bull slid backward, revealing a stairway cut out of the ground.

"I'm hoping you don't have some kind of gimp dungeon down there," said Flynn with a nervous laugh.

"Actually, I do, Flynn. If by 'gimp' you mean 'ambitious vigor.' Though I don't think you'll use the word 'dungeon' once you see it."

Jordache turned to Flynn. He looked into her eyes in a long gaze and then nodded.

The stairs led to a glass-walled elevator. Roughly hewn rock could be seen passing upward on the outside of the elevator as they descended multiple stories below ground.

The door opened to the sound of Donizetti's *Il Diluvio Universale* playing from warm, high-fidelity speakers. Noah and his guests stepped out.

"You have a lair?" said Flynn.

Klaven's lips left their grin and protruded as he nodded his head.

"Not a dungeon," said Jordache. "Definitely not a dungeon."

The entire two-story space was cut out of rock. Glass walls enclosed a conference room that overlooked the rest of the lair. The primary space featured workstations where programmers (well, mostly hackers to be specific) sipped energy drinks and clicked away at keyboards. Beyond them, as in the Too Soon Saloon, was an enormous screen Noah called "The Flood" displaying a bunch of computer data that scrolled at the same quick clip as the programmers typed. The only fixed figure on the screen was a small red tulip in the bottom right-hand corner. Above The Flood was a sign that read, "WISE AS SERPENTS, INNOCENT AS DOVES."

Noah put his thumbs in the straps of his overalls and motioned to the programmers with a nod. "The boys are welcome to use the saloon up in the barn after hours, but its main purpose is to serve as a decoy in case any bureaucrats come snooping around. Wouldn't even occur to most of them suits to dig deeper than poking around the saloon. I'd given 'em some quarters for the pinball machine and let 'em play giddy up on the mechanical bull, and they'd be good to go. One silver lining about the level of corruption we're seeing today is that it quickly leads to incompetence and weakness right on up the chain of command. That's buying us time because, throughout history, these folks always come after the farms. C'mon. follow me."

Noah led them past the programmers along the path of an underground stream that emerged from a cave-like opening in one part of the room and exited from another.

They passed a recreational area with weights, a pool, a hot tub, hydromassage chairs. Next was a library with a fireplace, couches, and reading tables with those sophisticated-looking green lampshade lights.

"The only thing you're missing here is a bald cat," said Flynn. "You don't have a bald cat, do you?"

"No bald cats. Got a mutt with a bit of mange running around somewhere though."

Noah led them down a hall with a long row of suites, each an elegant, minimalist space—a place to sleep, a place to study, a bathroom. He gave Flynn and Jordache a room to share and Klaven his own room.

After settling in, the three met with Noah in the conference room. Klaven was mesmerized by a slow trickling waterfall running down the wall in the corner of the room.

Jordache ran her hand along the grain of the natural cut of wood serving as a conference tabletop. It had swirls of shifting shades from blonde to chocolate and knots that drew her gaze inward as they seemed to carve out dimensions deeper than the thickness of the table.

"Gopherwood," said the farmer.

"Ah, well that makes sense, *Noah*. But I thought no one knew what kind of wood that is."

"I know," he said with a satisfied look.

"Well, it's beautiful."

"What are they working on?" asked Flynn, motioning to the programmers clicking away below.

"The Sons of Thunder? They're crunching numbers. Two numbers, to be specific. Ones and zeroes. They search, solve, and duplicate. At least that's what they tell me."

"You mean, you don't know what they're working on?"

"I'm a farmer. I help bring life out of the seed, though I know not how the life within the seed truly works. I suppose I'm doing the same with them . . . and with you. I'm not sure how this is all supposed to work together—but we have been brought together, so there's that. Some people use computers to control. The Sons of Thunder work to liberate."

Noah smiled at the sublime look on Klaven's face. "I can tell you're the intuitive one of the bunch, Klaven. What do you make of all of this?"

Klaven closed his eyes and nodded his head slowly. *"All that's golden is glitter,"* he sang to a familiar melody.

"What is that supposed to mean?" asked Flynn.

"Well, words can have inverse connotations . . ."

"Wait a minute—" said Flynn.

"You can travel by dual roads if you want to, but you'll shine on the narrow path," Klaven continued.

"He's just tweaking lyrics from 'Stairway to Heaven'!"

Noah put his hand on Klaven's shoulder. "This guy gets it. I think we go with this," he said addressing them all. "I'll keep farmin', the Sons of Thunder keep chasin' that binary code, and you keep plantin' tulips. We got this far on faith. I don't think we'll need to plot out our next move—I reckon it will simply present itself when its time comes."

•   •   •

Trapper and the mysterious blonde bobbed up and down to the rhythm of the elephant on which they rode. There was no fondue this time, but the mission was the same: Transfer a snow globe from the blonde's people to Trapper, who would get it to Hyden.

"Was this really necessary? Meeting on an elephant on safari?" said the blonde.

Trapper sat up straight, puffing out his bare chest. He insisted on dressing like Tarzan. Unfortunately, never having lifted a weight in his life and yet lifting many servings of fondue to his mouth did not give him a body that resembled anything like his animated hero. "My daddy said I can have this once The Great Exchange happens, so I wanted to check it out in person."

"This elephant? Your father is giving you an elephant?"

"No. Africa."

The blonde's eyebrows rose as she took in the huge plain on which they traveled: endless grass interrupted rarely by a marula tree, a pack of zebras and other wildlife here and there, and, in the far distance, mountains—a mere speck of the continent, of course. "All of it?"

Trapper smiled and nodded like a spoiled boy who received an oversized lollipop at the carnival. "The Big Cheese told me he's keeping all the snow globes now, instead of his normal ten percent cut. That's why I get Africa."

The elephant took a sudden turn and started running toward one of those few trees in the distance.

The elephant pilot, called a mahout, let out a panicky shriek. She pulled back on the reins, which did nothing to slow the elephant's gallop.

"Are you sure you know what you're doing up there?" said Trapper.

"Oh yes," said the mahout in the worst impression of a Chichewa accent ever. She turned around briefly to look at her two passengers. "The elephant goes where the elephant she goes. She will get tired soon."

The mahout was none other than Judy Ravioli in disguise. It cost her quite a few Pökermang cards to pay off Zeke's Wild Safari Tours so she could commandeer Trapper's reserved elephant. But Ace was bankrolling her mission, so black market coin was no problem. Mastering the techniques necessary to control an elephant in a one-hour mahout crash course shortly before Trapper's appointment—now that was a problem.

Fortunately for all three of them, the elephant made it to the marula tree and was quite pleased to munch on its yellow fruit.

Trapper plucked one of the fruits from the tree. "Are these edible for humans?" he asked the tour guide.

"Oh, those?" Judy said in her sad excuse for an accent. "*Pff.* Oh yes," she said, taking a wild guess. She immediately thought it would have been better to say *no* and be wrong than to say *yes* and be wrong, but what was done was done.

"Well, here you go," he said, handing the one he picked to Judy, then picking another one for himself and the blonde.

Judy winced as she bit into hers but was pleasantly surprised as the sweet, nutty juice of the fruit filled her mouth. (It would be several hours later before she would realize, to her great joy, that the fruit was indeed not poisonous.) She adjusted her shoulder bag to be sure the camera it concealed was still lined up behind her, capturing the conversation and actions of her riders.

"Well, this is as good of place as any," Trapper said to the blonde.

She reached into her bag and withdrew the snow globe.

Trapper grabbed it but then almost dropped it because his fingers were covered in marula juice. He regained his grip and looked at it with a frown. "Looks just like the other one." He placed the globe into one of the elephant's saddlebags, grabbed another fruit, and took a bite.

• • •

"*May you live in interesting times.* When I was a kid and heard that phrase was a back-handed curse, I didn't get it. Well, I get it now," Flynn said as he plopped a tulip bulb—one of thousands he personally planted by this point—into a small hole, covered it with dirt, and moved sideways to start on the next. All under a full midnight moon.

"Indeed," said Jordache, who patted the soil above her freshly-planted bulb.

Klaven and a large crew of ex-cons supervised by Ángel planted beyond them. Ángel had made a lot of friends while in the joint.

Flynn dropped his shovel. "Don't you think this could all be in vain?"

"*Vanity of vanities, saith the Preacher, vanity of vanities; all is vanity.*"

"Well, that helps with my calluses."

"Hand calluses—also vanity. If you're not willing to plant the seeds, or in this case the bulbs, you can be damn sure there'll be no harvest, Flynn."

"Just to be clear, though. This whole equity thing is going to lead to mass starvation. Maybe we should switch to planting, oh, I don't know, food, like Noah?"

"Well, fair enough. Technically, parts of the tulip are edible, though I get your point. But this has gone beyond mere biological survival. Our civilization has let its basement get disordered, and we think we can just go tidy it up a bit and all will be fine. It's like, guess again, Miss Sunshine. The rot runs deep. The Jungian shadow has risen, and it does not conform to logic. It devours unless it's confronted on its own terms."

"You're not saying to fight darkness with darkness?"

"The exact opposite. You expose hate with love; overcome the shadow with light. But it's going to take sacrifice, and a lot of it, to turn things around. People don't like sacrifice because it's painful. I tell them, *don't* sacrifice, and there will come a pain that feels like a Soviet gulag stuffed into a Nazi concentration camp and lit on fire."

"That's quite a visual there, honey."

Jordache stopped digging. "The shadow exists in the spiritual realm. This battle requires faith. Close your eyes, Flynn."

Flynn smirked at Jordache.

"No, really."

Flynn closed his eyes.

"Picture light pouring out, extinguishing the darkness."

Flynn started to smile. "I think I—"

"Okay, enough of that," Jordache said. "Back to digging, for faith without works is dead."

Flynn shook his head at his wife and jabbed his spade back into the ground.

"Not so fast. Agent Sanchez. Drop that spade."

The voice came from behind them from a man in a black suit—not a part of the tulip crew. He held up a badge identifying himself as an FBI officer. Several similarly dressed apparatchiks stood behind him.

"Where did you come from?" said Flynn.

"Walked up while you two were meditating, or whatever you were doing. Point is, I got a call that there was unauthorized planting on public property, and I'm here to stop it."

Jordache dropped her spade and stood up. "Unauthorized planting? And they sent the FBI for that?"

"Right. Normally, they'd send local cops. But you're both on multiple government watch lists due to your Fluttyr Quix flit implying that romantic love can be enjoyed between biological men and women. I'm not here to judge your sick body of work. I'm here to stop this planting."

"So, you hate Gaia and want a global apocalypse?" said Jordache, slipping a wink to Flynn.

"Sorry, I'm not following."

"Read the literature, Agent Sanchez. My work on panda psychopathology has been cited extensively as evidence for the causal link between minuscule increases in the Earth's temperature and the inability of pandas to achieve fulfilling relationships." She increased her volume so Agent Sanchez's crew could hear her words as well. "Ergo, we need to stop the climate from changing so that it can perpetually be at the exact temperature government-funded scientists say it should be. To do that, we need to remove carbon dioxide from the atmosphere. We're planting bulbs that produce green leafy plants which then absorb carbon dioxide and release oxygen. If you stop us, the fascists win, and the pandas die." Jordache squared off with Sanchez and brushed the soil from her hands. She pulled her phone out of her pocket and displayed a gif of a baby panda drawn anime style with extra-large, teary eyes, fanning itself with a bamboo stem and the caption: *I'm so hot.* "Now, you don't want me to call the press and let them know that your agency is pushing fascist, panda-murdering policies, do you?"

Sanchez looked nervously at the other agents. "I just said we got a call. Take it easy. We didn't know you were with us."

Flynn played along with his wife's ruse, letting out an exaggerated huff. "Our Quix are deep double-fakeouts. You must not be high enough in the command chain to have been briefed on the true nature of our work. Can we get back to saving the world?"

"Oh. Of course," said Sanchez, handing them each a card. "Please do. If anyone bothers you, you give me a call."

Sanchez turned and scooted his agents off into the night with him.

Jordache and Flynn shared a quick knuckle-bump and got back to work . . . Dig. Drop in tulip bulb. Bury tulip bulb. Have a brief, cryptic exchange with Klaven. Dig. Drop in tulip bulb. Bury tulip bulb. Have a brief, cryptic exchange with Klaven . . . And on and on into the night . . .

10

Miss O'Jenny & The Big Cheese

Z'Bendy looked around the table in the Presidential bowling lane as 50s doo-wop music played in the background. They let Hyden pick the music. "Look, someone or some group within the Deep State has gone rogue. That's obvious. But it still seems that they're on our side."

"That's *zour* side," said DiCherubino. "You must use *zour* if I'm included in your collective pronoun. Stop genociding me. You should know this. You're trans, too." She swatted him on the arm.

"I'm sorry, πü≈'re right," he gagged. "My wrong pronoun use was hateful violence, but πü≈r hitting my arm was helpful speech. Like I was saying, it seems that they're on zour side. They've gotten the masses fighting in the streets much faster than ze could accomplish on zour own—and when the masses are fighting each other, they're not paying attention to what ze're up to."

"Ze're heading in the right direction," said DiCherubino. "The pathetic little bartering networks they set up will only last so long, and the chaos is getting to people."

"I've got it," said Blasé. "Why don't ze set up federally monitored bartering stations until ze resolve the equity virus? Could reduce some of the chaos."

"Blasé. The chaos is zour friend. The more chaotic they get, the more they need zux to provide order. Ze still have the infrastructure to 'solve' their problems. Ze've been setting up camps for years in case of an 'emergency.' Well, this is the emergency ze've been waiting for. Hungry people will abandon their homes and towns and swarm the camps for food. From there, ze'll organize them into densely populated and heavily regulated work communities. Once ze cram them into . . . let'x call them 'Sexy Serf Sanctuaries' for marketing purposes, ze can make sure they don't travel or use air conditioners, heaters, or gas stoves. And lots of bug eating," zhe said with a smirk.

"Oh, that's right—you said that was to save the planet from Climate Change™," said zer obtuse comrade.

"Right, Climate Change™," said DiCherubino as zhe shot a *could this guy really be that dumb?* look to Z'Bendy. "Bottom line is, with race and class gone, ze have one weapon left: sex."

"Sex?" said Blasé.

"Here's the problem: Ze've lost too many police and military due to Equity, so, though ze've got the weapons, ze lack the person-power. Ze need the changes ze're pushing to seem voluntary—and ze need attacks ze can't make zourxelves to come from the masses. But, ze've been losing the support of married women with children. If ze can't get them to avoid marriage and abort their children, they're goners; and that means ze're goners."

"But ze do convert many of their children to zour worldview if they let them be born," said Blasé.

"Only a moderate percentage of the ones in public schools and the elite private schools though. It's not enough. Divide and conquer is the only way. Race is gone. Inequity is gone. So, ze turn up the heat on zour attack on misogyny—"

"Miss O'Jenny, a real cutie. Irish lass," Hyden muttered. "My first kiss out back of the schoolhouse when we were kids. True story . . ."

"Like Xi was saying, ze turn up the heat on zour attack on misogyny, which will add conflict between men and women and families. As families fail, government becomes mommy and daddy."

"This calls for a Presidential Presser," said Z'Bendy.

"Exactly. Let'x do it at the upcoming unveiling." With that, DiCherubino called an end to the meeting.

"Let's go, Mr. President," said Blasé.

"You cats beat feet. I'm gonna stay down here and doo-wop for a few."

"You think he's okay here by himself?" Blasé whispered to Z'Bendy.

Z'Bendy grabbed a remote control with a single button on it and handed it to Hyden. "Hit this if you need anything, Mr. President, and the Secret Service will be right down."

"Got it, Daddy-O. Toodles."

The moment they left the alley, Hyden popped to his feet, locked the door, pulled his sleeve up, and quickly tapped a message into his smartwatch.

All signs of dementia were gone.

Second later there was a knock from a side door.

He whipped the door open.

Trapper moseyed in wearing wet board shorts and nothing else. Fondue dribbled down his face, missing the napkin in his hand. In his other hand, he held a reusable grocery bag.

"Quickly," Hyden said. "The Secret Service will be checking on me soon." He gave Trapper an aggressive tug to get him fully in the room and then closed the door. "Well?" he said.

Trapper reached into the bag, pulled out the snow globe, and handed it to Hyden.

His hands cradled the snow globe as if it was a baby. His face brightened.

"Good work, son. Good work. Though it's got something sticky all over it." Hyden's eyes didn't leave the snow globe.

"It's juice from some marula fruit."

"Right. Doesn't really matter anyway. Scoot along now. Go play in the pool . . . or whatever."

"I still get Africa, right, Daddy?"

"Yes . . . well, just make sure you get that third snow globe." With that, Hyden hustled Trapper out the door and closed it behind him.

Hyden walked to the bowling lane and gazed into the globe, past the lead glass, and into the ceramic scene. It was a shrine, but in place of an altar was a computer. And on top of the computer . . . a banana? Yes, a banana.

He lifted the orb above his head and then dashed it into the hard wood below. It exploded upon contact, sending shards of glass and ceramics and bone-chip *snow* and splashes of fetid water in all directions. He picked the miniature banana up out of the gutter and walked over to the bowling lane's bar.

He peeled a rubbery coat of paint off the banana and pulled out a tiny scroll of translucent paper, which he laid out on the counter. He pulled another similar-looking scroll out of the pocket in his Hyden Pinz bowling shirt and laid it on top of the new one. Together, the two scrolls formed a series of elaborate symbols as if they were writing, though they were not letters or numerals of any known language. They were clearly made to fit together, but they looked incomplete, as well, as though there was more to the symbols than these two scrolls revealed.

Hyden's eyes flashed an ominous red, like eyes appear in a photo when light reflects off the back of their retinae.

He placed the scrolls in his pocket, sat down, and pressed the button on the remote Z'Bendy left with him.

The Secret Service entered the room seconds later. Hyden lifted his hand and pointed with fake frailty toward the lane with the destroyed snow globe. "Daddy made a boom boom."

•   •   •

"The final phase of the Envision Protocol is ready," said Eppy in a Züm meeting with OAC and Von Cappuccino.

For some reason, OAC had her phone camera pointing at her chest.

"We can't see your face, OAC. Can you adjust your camera?"

"Sure," she said. Instead of raising the phone's angle, she hit the selfie button, or in this case the un-selfie button. Instead of her chest, Eppy and Von Cappuccino now looked at her emaciated "vegan" cat, Stalin. Stalin tried to meow a plea for help, and for meat, but all that came out was air.

"As I was saying," Eppy continued as he swiped away the visual of OAC's abused cat on his phone screen, "the final phase of the Envision Protocol is ready, but we can't risk enacting it remotely. We have to meet face-to-face with Anonymous."

"The person who writes all those letters to the editor at the newspaper?" said OAC.

Von Cappuccino sighed and shook his head, causing the tassel of his tam to quiver. "No, the hacker."

"Oh."

"Pack your cowboy hats, kids," said Eppy. "We're going to Dallas, Texas."

•   •   •

"Without further ado, release the Kraken," said Hyden. He waved his hand before an enormous object covered with a Progress Flag tarp behind him on Gaslight Island.

"I'm kidding," he whispered into the mic. "This is better than a Kraken. It is the finished statue that you, the American people, by your participation in our mandatory gold confiscation program, made possible. You can't eat beef anymore, thanks to me, but when you feel the stirring of hunger within, you can, with hope in your heart, behold . . . the Golden Calf."

The live news coverage flashed an undetectably fast polarized graphic of the word "EVIL" on the screen as Hyden spoke—the news feed had been hacked.

DiCherubino and Z'Bendy smiled at zeach xother. "He's doing a great job with the teleprompter today," zhe said. "Xi think those stimulants ze popped in his coffee are kicking in."

The gaudy tarp fell revealing a gargantuan golden calf where the Statue of Liberty once stood. Because the Hyden Administration did not include merit or talent in the qualifications of the sculptor they had hired to make the calf, the statue looked more like that which an animal would excrete than an actual animal. The gender-fluid, Indo-Satanic vampire-self "artist" stood proudly before his work, though it was unclear if he was near the rear or head of the beast.

"Give me your transgendered," shouted Hyden, "your antiracist, your huddled drag queens yearning to be libertine with children. I lift my lamp beside the Golden Calf."

A crowd of tens, mostly drag queens and preschoolers with their Munchausen Syndrome by Proxy-afflicted mothers, clapped.

"As much as we have to celebrate today," said Hyden. "One race. Pause for applause. Equity. Pause for applause. This real dandy calf back here. Pause for applause. And yes, I do rhyme all the time."

"πü≈ spoke too soon," whispered Z'Bendy. "He's reading the directions from the teleprompter and improvising again."

Hyden continued. "We still have one major issue to tackle. I'd like to invite Public Health Czar Timmy Fazi to say a few words about the most ominous menace we all face."

A trollish-looking man walked up to the mic as he tried to determine which of the multiple cameras pointing in his direction was live. He found the one with the red light and flashed an ingratiating grin. "I just want to say to the American people that your health is the primary concern of the Hyden Administration. I mean, look at the way we helped you survive that last virus we weaponized in a lab by forcing you to stay home, away from the sunshine and fresh air, while we mandated you to take experimental vaccines. If that doesn't say competence and care, I don't know what does."

Another polarized graphic flashed on the news feeds: "CHARLATAN."

"But we have something more pernicious than a lab-created virus in our midst," continued Fazi, "and that is straight men."

Hyden wandered over to the statue while Fazi spoke and started sniffing the calf. He shook his head disappointedly as Z'Bendy escorted him back to his spot on the stage.

"You might be wondering how straight men are a health threat," Fazi continued. "Fortunately, I am Science, so I will explain it to you. Straight men are helping straight women make babies through a disgusting practice called heterosexual sex. There are two terrible outcomes of this sex and the babies it produces: First, it makes non-heterosexual sex acts seem inferior, which leads some people to feel bad, and because they feel bad, these heterosexual men are therefore committing hate crimes when they consensually mate with their wives; second—you guessed it—babies cause Climate Change™. So, we must attack straight men to fight hate and to save the planet."

The drag queens and Munchausen mommies in the audience cheered and made catcalls directed at Fazi to show their approval.

Hyden returned to the podium, hugging his folder especially close to his chest. "Daddy was a convict for most of his adult life, but he was the good kind of convict. Voted 'Most Valuable Player' during the Attica prison riot back in '71. Anyway, he used to say, Moey, that's what my dad called me."

Z'Bendy started to walk over to stop him, but DiCherubino put her hand on his shoulder. "Let'x see where he's going with this."

"Moey, when you see an injustice, what you do is, you grab a bar of soap. Not one of these dainty hotel soaps either, but a nice big bar of prison-issue soap. You wrap it in a washcloth, and you pummel that injustice."

DiCherubino nodded zer head at Z'Bendy. "Not bad."

"And I know what you're thinking," Hyden continued. "How are we gonna know who the straight men are? Well, problem solved." He opened his folder and moved his copy of *The Little Engine That Could* aside. Pulled out an eight-and-a-half by eleven-inch glossy of Olivia Newton-John roller-skating in the movie *Xanadu*. "You show a fella this, and if you see a sparkle in his eye, you know you got yourself one of those patriarchal, heteronormative, low down and dirty, fascistic, *straight men*," he spit out the words. "Now, I'm not joking. This'll work. Dead serious. I'm not joking. Dead serious, man . . ." Hyden faked one of his verbal loops, and Z'Bendy quickly escorted him aside. A naked drag queen with Satan horns and tail walked to the podium to read an obscene story to the children gathered for the event. Another graphic, undetected by the conscious minds that watched on TV and devices, flashed: "DEPRAVED."

Blasé covered the spectacle live on SNN with Alouette Jean-Luc le Pew as his guest. Blasé was comfortable with Hyden's new proclamation, for the photo of Olivia Newton-John would cause no stir in his loins, but he frowned. "Isn't Hyden a straight man? I mean, he has a wife, Gretchen Hyden, Esquire."

Le Pew laughed and shook her head. "You must have missed the President's announcement on National Coming Out Day that he is now and has always been a lesbian."

"But they have children."

"Lesbians impregnate other lesbians all the time, Blasé. To say otherwise is to commit voluntary personslaughter on marginalized people. You might want to have Dr. Fazi on your show to explain the birds and bees to you and visit one of our thousands of conveniently-located re-education camps."

Blasé nodded. "You're probably right." He put his finger to his earpiece. "We're getting reports of something odd happening in major cities across America. We're going live to West Los Angeles."

SNN's LA correspondent stood at a busy intersection with homeless encampments and people shooting drugs in the background. "It appears that as President Hyden was speaking from Gaslight Island just moments ago, pallets of soap and washcloths, along with photos of Olivia Newton-John skating in the movie *Xanadu*, appeared in urban areas across the US. No one knows who provided these materials."

"Odd," said Blasé, with consternation in his voice. A man with bright pink hair, high heels, and a beard could be seen behind the SNN correspondent grabbing a bar of soap, washcloth, and Olivia Newton-John photo. He held the photo up to several different men before one's eyes apparently sparkled. The pink-haired man beat the straight man to the ground with the washcloth-wrapped soap.

"As you can see, mostly peaceful here, Blasé," said the correspondent as the pink-haired man approached him. The correspondent tried to avert his eyes from the photo, but he could not—for the allure of Olivia Newton-John's image was just too strong.

The moment before the bar of soap met the skull of the correspondent, a wave of multi-colored, wavy lines overtook the screens tuned to the SNN feed. The lines faded as subliminal shots of a red tulip flashed on and off like a strobe before disappearing. And there on SNN appeared the determined eyes and the confident jaw jutting out from the face of none other than ... Ace MacDonald. "I'm ba-ack," he said in a taunting delivery.

Jordache, Flynn, Klaven, and Noah looked at the six-foot-tall face of the former President on the big screen at the Too Soon Saloon. Navy blue suit with a red tie. Dyed blonde-orange hair shellacked into a hirsute helmet. Prison teardrop tattoo below his left eye. MacDonald stood in a secret location. Behind him, there was a United States Flag topped with a preserved bald eagle and life-sized cutout photos of John Wayne, *Jailhouse Rock* Elvis, and Sylvester Stallone in character as John Rambo.

No one at the Saloon said a word, except for Klaven who whooped out a "Yeehaw!" as he rode the mechanical bull at slow speed.

"Before the major corrupt networks cut off my speech," said MacDonald, "I want to tell you all, this video has already been posted in its entirety on Fluttyr. Terrific video really. It will be one of the best-rated and most-shared flits of all time."

Fluttyr had been purchased by eccentric billionaire Oakley Spice for an absurd amount of money shortly before Jordache and Flynn started Lobster Flex. Spice had made his billions in beer koozies that featured clever sayings like, "Step aside coffee, this is a job for beer," and "In beer's defense, I've done some pretty dumb stuff while sober, too." He bought Fluttyr because of his love of cat gifs and also so he could restore free speech to the platform, which had been controlled, prior to his purchase, by the CIA. But mainly because of the cat gifs.

The SNN transmission disappeared from the Too Soon Saloon's screen.

Jordache turned to Noah. "Can you pull up Fluttyr on your screen?"

Noah tapped an app on his phone, and the President appeared.

MacDonald continued. "While I was a political prisoner in Guantanamo Bay, Cuba, my trusted attorney and crack investigator, Judy Ravioli ... she really is a tremendous investigator, folks—people say she's the best, and she really is."

The camera angle widened to show Judy Ravioli standing with MacDonald. Judy blushed at MacDonald's praise and, with her sleeve, wiped some hastily applied hair dye that was dripping down her temple. "Thank you, Ace."

"Judy has been tracking the corrupt and reckless behavior of my arch nemesis, Moe STEALINETTE Hyden," he said, cranking up the volume and guttural growl on the President's middle name. "Are you getting this, Scribe?"

The camera view widened further to reveal MacDonald's former cellmate, The Scribe, standing to his other side.

The Scribe looked up briefly from the roll of toilet paper on which he transcribed MacDonald's every word. "Yes, sir."

"Thank you, Scribe." He faced the camera again. "He doesn't miss a jot or tittle. First thing we did upon our release was get a publishing deal for my prison-drafted memoir, *My Struggle*, available on the black market this fall. Folks, it's going to be a bestseller. Having it printed on toilet paper rolls, just like it was composed. No edits— from my mind to you, the people who love me, the American people. All books will be written on toilet paper in the future after you all read my unprecedented masterpiece, you'll see.

"But I'm not here to talk about toilet paper, folks. I'm here to tell you about the Deep Deep State. You all know about the Deep State. That's who conspired to have me, the greatest President since . . . well, they conspired to have the greatest President of all time locked up. The Deep State are vicious sharks. It was all trumped-up charges. 'Ebony and Ivory' actually is my number one favorite song of all time, but I wouldn't give those bastards the pleasure of hearing me say it was so. In America, everyone is free to lie if they want to, especially about their favorite song. But the point is, there's another level below the Deep State, and that's the Deep Deep State. And they're the ones pulling all the strings like a . . . well, Metallica put it best, they're the 'Master of Puppets.'

Great song, by the way, folks. Found myself humming it often in the shower at GITMO. Drove the terrorist inmates nuts. But the Deep Deep State. They're evil. Dividing people and filling them with fear to control them. They want to turn you back into serfs or worse. Much much worse. If I don't stop them, they'll have you all living in hot cubicles and eating bugs in no time at all. And worst of all, they come up with all of those hand symbols pop stars and world leaders use in photos. You know . . ." he moved his hand over his chest, between the buttons of his blazer, like Napoleon, then put it over one eye to demonstrate. "What a bunch of sickos. They're really sick, folks. And Hyden is the worst of the bunch. Judy infiltrated his secret little club of world leaders called The Secret Society. Can you believe that? A secret society called The Secret Society. Real branding geniuses, these guys," he said with a sarcastic huff. "What a bunch of losers. So, Judy infiltrates their organization and sees what they're up to. They're eating buffalo-style baby condor wings at their cocktail hour, watching cabaret shows starring tutu-wearing otters. I'm telling you, real perverted stuff.

"But the important thing is, we've got Hyden. Caught him in a snow globe-for-influence scheme. Judy traced his corrupt son, Trapper. So corrupt. And a real slob, too. This guy eats like a pig. I haven't seen it myself, but very knowledgeable people tell me he eats like a pig. Judy watched him receive snow globes in Europe and Africa. The kid's as stupid as his father. Left evidence of where each meeting was to take place. Judy went deep undercover for a snow globe handoff set up by Trapper, and get this. Go ahead, Judy."

"Had to go all the way to the Great Wall of China to intercept the latest payoff Trapper was supposed to receive," Judy said as she lifted the third snow globe out of her purse.

"She dressed up as a rickshaw driver," MacDonald said. "I told her that was very racist, and I didn't approve of it, but she's a real fighter, Judy. Did it anyway. Judy's got video evidence of Trapper accepting two other snow globes for 'The Big Cheese,' as he refers to his dad. Big league corruption with the Hyden Crime Family. Corruption, frankly, like we've never seen before."

MacDonald grabbed the sides of the podium. "We all know our justice system is rigged by Hyden and his cronies, so this trial will take place in the court of public opinion." He looked directly into the camera. "I'm talking to you now, Hyden. You've got one day to resign, or I'm making all of the dirt I have on you public."

MacDonald lifted his finger to his teardrop tattoo. "Ace out."

11

Novus Ordo Seclorum

As planned by the Hyden Administration, brutality erupted in the streets. Family Friendly Drag Queens®; beta males who realized their moment to act on their resentment of masculine men had arrived; women who had fallen for the pay gap myth—all viciously gave straight men the prison soap beat down every chance they could. But now the Hyden Administration had something else to worry about—what did Ace MacDonald have up his sleeve?

"It's your favorite, Mr. President," said Z'Bendy, "rainbow sherbet."

Hyden took a bite of sherbet as Blasé threw a strike in the Presidential bowling lane.

"If they take down the old man," said DiCherubino, "ze're going down with him. But with zour Deep State and Deep Deep State staffing so low due to Equity, ze haven't been able to track down MacDonald to . . . uh . . . take him out the old-fashioned way."

"Look—" said Hyden.

"The President wants to bowl, Blasé," said Z'Bendy. "Can you—"

"Let's cut the crap," said Hyden, the glazed look in his eyes replaced by a sharp stare. Not an intelligent stare. Even when he wasn't faking senility, Moe wasn't that bright, but gone was the addled, gaspy tremble in his voice. "Things just got serious with this accusation, and I can't count on πü≈ nincompoops to resolve it."

Blasé dropped his sherbet. Xeverywyne's but Hyden's mouths and eyes opened wide. "You mean . . . all this time . . . you—"

"Yes, I've been faking advanced dementia all this time. The Left has become so detached from reality that there was no better way to rise to power than to appear as an empty vessel. And πü≈ three swooped right in to fill that vessel with the nonsense πü≈ wanted to push on the public while I orchestrated my true agenda."

DiCherubino gulped as perspiration appeared on zer otherwise preternaturally confident brow.

"Don't worry, I'll still be using πü≈," gagged Hyden. "πü≈ clearly have no integrity or values, which means πü≈ continue to be useful to me."

Blasé pushed his shoulders back and straightened the lapels of his sharkskin blazer. "I value fashion," he said with a pursed mouth.

"Right," said Hyden. "And ze'll need you to use your fashionable smarm to sell what ze're about to do."

"And what exactly is that?" asked DiCherubino.

"MacDonald was right about one thing. I have been collecting a series of snow globes, but it's not because of my snow globe addiction. I kicked that habit cold turkey years ago when Gretchen Hyden, Esquire, wouldn't let me use any more shelf space for my collection. The snow globes Trapper has been acquiring are used to pass codes. MacDonald has no clue about what The Secret Society is planning."

"The Secret Society? So, he was right about that?" said Z'Bendy.

"The Secret Society is an order of the most powerful leaders and influencers in the world. Real exclusive club." Hyden smiled like a proud little boy. "I'm on our lodge's Special Events and Parties Committee. But like I was saying, The Secret Society is launching our next phase of the *Novus Ordo Seclorum*. No clue what those words translate to—one of the fellas in The Secret Society said he nicked the phrase from our dollar bill. But the plan is that there will be one god-king for each region of the world. I'm taking North and South America, Trapper's getting Africa, and there are others lined up for Asia and Europe. If πü≈ stay in line, I'll let πü≈ three split up Australia. None of the other god-kings wanted that one."

"I call Sydney!" said Blasé.

"Oh, shut up," snapped DiCherubino.

Blasé's face dropped into a pout.

"Was The Secret Society behind the Yucky Race Erasure and Equity?" asked Z'Bendy.

"No, that wasn't us, but whoever it was couldn't do more to help accomplish our plan. Their actions in combination with πü≈r manipulation of people to violence and crime . . ." Hyden paused to wipe his misty eyes. "Just fills the heart with lust for power."

"You already have power," said Z'Bendy. "Why this next phase?"

"Living as the President of a free country is nice. Living as a despot wielding unrestrained authority, with no need for a public façade of decency, will be . . ." He paused to draw in a deep breath through his nose. "Scrumptious."

DiCherubino could feel saliva filling zer mouth at the President's words.

"You mentioned a code. How does a code accomplish this?" asked Z'Bendy.

"Empires fell in the past because they couldn't manage the minutia it takes to truly tyrannize people once the empires grew beyond a certain size. But today, the world is managed using a series of computer-controlled systems. It's so diabolically clever . . ." he snickered. "Being leader of the most powerful nation, I have been selected by The Secret Society to implement The Great Exchange. Consolidate the various computer systems into what we call 'The Grid,' and we control the world—financially, militarily, totally."

"This does sound nice and totalitarian, which I'm all about," said DiCherubino, "but you still have to control The Grid. Won't that lead to the same problem the empires had in the past?"

"That's where the 'Exchange' part comes in." The edges of Hyden's mouth spread into a maniacal grin. "AI. Artificial Intelligence." He pulled three scrolls from his pocket. "Each of these contains part of a code that key world leaders, members of The Secret Society, have provided. Trapper delivered the first two via snow globe. One of them is mine. And that . . . Ace MacDonald," he said his name as if was profanity, "has the fourth and final scroll. He has no clue what power he holds within that snow globe, the fool. The Grid is on the verge of being completed. When the scrolls are combined, they will form the code that will be used to deliver control of The Grid to a new AI program developed by the Deep Deep State. Then the god-kings will be free to really get turned up!"

Z'Bendy shook his head at the President's use of a term about three generations removed from his age. "That's 'turnt up,' Mr. President. Or, if you really want to sound street, just 'turnt.' No preposition needed whatsoever."

"Turn it up, turnt it up, whatever. The bottom line is, ze'll make the gladiator games of Rome look like children's tea parties!"

"That does sound like fun," said Blasé. "But, just to clarify, part of our decline to total decadence can include actual tea parties, correct?"

Blasé was ignored. It perpetually crushed him that his "middle-child, always the overlooked one" status growing up followed him into his adult relationships.

"Xi have one question," said DiCherubino. "What's to keep the Artificial Intelligence from getting rid of the god-kings?"

"Do πü≈ take us for fools? We have that covered. We met this real neat guy about a year ago. Name's Damien.

A European prince. Charming. Handsome as the dickens. And resilient! The guy was mortally wounded while demonstrating his sword-swallowing skills at one of our parties—the sword was on fire and everything—then he totally healed, right in front of us. Anyway, Damien's not really part of The Great Exchange, but he offered to monitor the AI for us in a totally neutral fashion to make sure it doesn't get any wacky impulses toward power and dominance of its own."

"And how are you going to trust Damien?" said DiCherubino.

"πü≈ know, Raven, πü≈ really are a buzzkill. I'll bet πü≈ were the kid that threw a party in high school and then called the cops on πü≈r own party because no one was talking to πü≈."

A small tear fell down DiCherubino's cheek.

"The Secret Society operates via occultic practices," said Hyden. "We saw in a conjuring that the one to control the AI would have a birthmark of three 9s. Well, lo and behold, Damien dropped trou," Hyden chuckled as he spoke. "That cut-up! We were all doing the Macarena, and he just mooned us during the chorus to get a laugh. Had us rolling! Anyway, right there on his left cheek was the mark."

"Are you sure those were 9s and not—" Z'Bendy said before he was jarred in the ribs by DiCherubino's elbow, which was in turn pushed by Blyx. The demon was running late and just arrived to the meeting.

"Yep, three 9s," said Hyden. "Had to do a handstand to make 'em out but saw 'em with my own eyes."

"So, how are ze going to get that snow globe from MacDonald?" asked Z'Bendy.

"Easy," said Hyden. "Via his greatest weakness. His ego."

"But how are ze going to find him?" said DiCherubino. "Ze've had the few Deep State and Deep Deep State agents still on the payroll trying to find him, but he's eluded zux."

"Have πü≈ tried calling him?" Hyden said with a cocky huff. He walked to the ice cream bar behind them. Reached under the sink and tugged on something that made a tearing sound as it separated from the duct tape holding it in place. He lifted his hand revealing a flip-phone. "MacDonald and I each have burner phones. It's a President thing in case a current President needs to reach a former President off the record and out of the public space. Got MacDonald on speed dial."

Hyden hit number one and "call" on his phone. After a few rings . . . "Ace here."

"It's Moe. Got you on speaker."

"That's fine."

"So, you finally got the goods on me, Ace."

"You knew the day would come, Moe. I am relentless. Like a pit bull with a mailman's Achilles tendon in his jaws. Ace don't let go."

"Technically, you committed blackmail before the world when you said you would reveal the dirt you have on me unless I resign. But I recently ended crime, so we can't charge you with anything. Guess you found the loophole there."

"Unforced error on that move, Moe. As was freeing all prisoners, when one of those prisoners was me."

"Well, what can I say?" said Hyden. He put his hand over the mic and looked at the others in the room with a quiet *hee hee* escaping his mouth before continuing. "I know you will love hearing this. You win, Ace."

"I always win, Moe. I thought when I was a kid and always winning then that I might someday tire of winning. But guess what?"

"What?" said Hyden.

"Still not tired of winning. Not by a long shot. Sometimes I wonder if it's winning I like or if it's just making other people, as a consequence of my victory, losers. Both are delightful, but it's the winning I love most."

"There's one thing, Ace."

"What is it, Moe? No monkey business here. I won fair and square and expect your resignation forthwith."

"Well, Ace. You beat me because you knew I had a weakness for snow globes. You saw that snow globes would be the source of my undoing, and using your unparalleled strategic mind, you brought me down."

Hyden put his hand over the phone's mic again. "Am I laying it on too thick?" he said with tears of glee welling up in his eyes.

"Not possible," said Z'Bendy.

"I'm listening," said Ace.

Hyden continued, "You know what I'm going to say."

"You want the snow globe."

A long dramatic pause. "Of course, Ace. Well, I don't want the snow globe. I . . . I need the snow globe."

"You are a real pathetic loser, Moe. But sure, I've got the snow globe right here." He flicked it loudly with his finger so Hyden could hear it.

"Oh, do be careful with it, Ace. It's precious. To me."

"You resign. I'll give you the snow globe."

"I'll do you one better. We'll meet in person. I'll give you my handwritten letter of resignation—so you can be the one to share it with the press in triumph—and you hand off the snow globe."

"I like that. I'll come to the White House—my rightful home before it was stolen from me."

"No, not there. The Deep Deep State would just nab you the second you arrived. We meet at The Place."

"The Place?"

"The Place."

"Alright, Moe. I'll be there. Tomorrow at dawn."

12

Showdown

The planting phase of Operation Tulip had drawn to a close. Jordache, Flynn, Klaven, Ángel, and Ángel's crew now gathered nightly to tend to their garden. The plants had sprouted but not bloomed.

They walked the grounds in and around Dealey Plaza—Founders Plaza, Martyr's Park, and open spaces surrounding the Trinity River.

In normal times, the city would have mowed down the unauthorized plants—even if they were green and leafy and Climate Change™-combatting. But these weren't normal times. Equity meant that no city could find enough employees for regular maintenance—water and waste services were inconsistent; blackouts were common. This little portion of Dallas was one of the few areas in the country not overrun by uncut grass, weeds, and garbage—and it was all thanks to Operation Tulip and the care these "gardeners" gave to the space.

Jordache, Flynn, and Klaven sat down on the grassy knoll as dawn approached. Ángel was with them, but he stood, as he did not want to soil his immaculate white clothes.

Flynn smiled at the view of green leaves and closed flowers of the thousands of tulips they had planted. "I still don't know what this is all for, but it is kind of beautiful."

The Plaza was always deserted at this time of day, but they heard footsteps and voices coming from behind them.

"We look pretty ridiculous in these getups," mumbled Von Cappuccino. Like his two co-stooges, he was dressed head to toe in black. He even donned a black tam with a black tassel on top of his masked face.

"I told you," whispered Eppy, "we'll be safest if we dress as Antifa since they're the Deep State's unofficial *street* police.

"I thought we were dressed as ninjas," OAC moped.

"You can be a ninja, OAC. We'll be Antifa," said Eppy.

She pumped her fist. "Yes!"

"Ninjas are silent," said Von Cappuccino, his eyes narrowing in the slit in his mask.

"Can we help you?" asked Jordache, as the stooges were so close, she could have reached out and touched them.

Eppy put his hand to his chest. "Oh! We didn't see you there. Must be the masks. Sorry about that. Actually, you can help. Can you point us in the direction of the Book Depository?"

"If it was a snake, it would'a bit you," said Flynn. "It's right back there. You must have passed it on the way here."

"I told you that was it," said Von Cappuccino.

"Great, thank you," said Eppy. He gave a hand signal to his partners, and they turned to head back in the direction from which they had arrived at the knoll.

OAC looked over her shoulder. "Yes, thank you, guys and gal," she said with a snicker. "At least for now."

"Shh," said Von Cappuccino. "Don't give it away."

"I wonder what they're up to," said Jordache as the bickering voices of Von Cappuccino and OAC trailed off in their exit.

"Feds?" said Flynn.

"I'm pretty sure."

Klaven's grin spread across more of his face than usual as he tapped his watch.

"Yeah, we probably should head out of here," said Jordache. "Sun will be rising soon."

"I'm not pointing at the time," Klaven said in a teasing tone.

Flynn grabbed his wrist. "It says the 7th, if that's what you're getting at, Klaven. And that's incorrect, by the way."

"Even a broken calendar is right once a month."

"Wait a minute," said Jordache. "She grabbed her phone. Today is April 15th."

"The Ideas of April," said Flynn.

"Reality provides the interpretation . . . today," said Ángel, harkening back to his prophecy from months ago.

"Should we be looking for your circular sign?" said Flynn as he drew the shape into the air with his finger.

"You will not need to look, though you will want to look away." Ángel made a single clicking sound with his mouth. Upon hearing this, his crew dispersed, seeming to vanish into the surrounding shrubs and trees.

The sun had still not risen, but the glow of the horizon revealed the silhouette of a person in a trench coat rolling a churro cart into Dealey Plaza.

A group of eleven people approached on foot to the right and a group of three to the left.

"Maybe we should get back to the farm?" asked Jordache.

"But then we'd miss him," said Klaven.

"Miss who?" said Flynn.

Klaven sang, *"The one who sings with graceful lilting taste."*

"Another cryptic Led Zeppelin reference," said Flynn, shaking his head. "You know I love a good joke, but this isn't the time for riddles."

"I'm saying there's a Scot coming. You know, lilting. It's like the Scotch version of scat . . . It's not as fun if I have to explain it, Flynn."

"Well, thanks for the clarity, Klaven. I know exactly what's happening now."

Ángel motioned with his head, and the four of them scooted behind a wooden fence at the top of the hill. They huddled together and looked through breaks in the slats.

The two approaching groups squared off on the grassy knoll.

On one side it was Hyden, DiCherubino, Z'Bendy, Blasé, Trapper, and six secret service officers.

On the other, it was Ace MacDonald, Judy Ravioli, and The Scribe.

Oddly enough, MacDonald held a bowling ball bag, and Hyden held a single bowling pin.

Meanwhile, Eppy, OAC, and Von Cappuccino entered the sixth floor of what was once the Texas School Book Depository Company. The sixth floor of the building was now a museum with memorabilia related to the assassination of JFK. Though, that was actually a cover for the Deep Deep State, which used the sixth floor for its quarterly meetings as well as for its annual Ugly Sweater Party. They liked the vibe there and enjoyed the artifacts in the space more as a monument to their power than as a museum. This location also made for the perfect headquarters for hacker Anonymous's operations, where he could hide in plain sight doing "IT" work for the museum and at the same time easily coordinate with the Deep Deep State.

Blyx's three stooges approached the desk of Anonymous, who clicked away on a keyboard. He swiveled his chair in their direction, though his face was hidden behind a Guy Fawkes mask.

"You mean, you actually wear that while you're hacking?" said Eppy.

"Yeah," he said in a geeky monotone. "Helps me get in the mood for hijinks."

"Well," said Eppy, "you have done a great service helping us with The Great Race Blender and Equity. As you've probably seen, it really has made the world so much more fair and exciting."

"I'm about ready to clock out. What have you got?"

"This is the final act of our mission."

Anonymous put his hand out.

Von Cappuccino pulled a slip of paper out of his pocket. As he extended his hand, OAC swiped it. "I want to be the one, I want to be the one."

"But I discovered the last part of the equation," whined Von Cappuccino.

"Oh, let her give it to him," said Eppy. "That equation was given to you in a dream."

Anonymous clicked away on his keyboard. The Wardenclyffe Towers at the Earth's two poles awakened—digital decks flashing lights, metallic dishes winding up into smooth revolutions, computers leaving sleep mode and awaiting further instructions.

Blyx looked around with a conceited smirk at the countless demons surrounding him in the room. His pyramid had greatly expanded as elites used The Great Race Blender and Equity to produce levels of evil within the general public not seen since the communist struggle sessions of the past century—oh, how the demons loved those struggle sessions! There were so many demons in the JFK museum, they poured out of the sixth floor of the building and into the plaza below.

MacDonald and Hyden told their people to stay in place as the two men approached each other, slow and easy. They were pretty old, after all.

Trapper stepped backward so as not to get the attention of his father's team and made his way toward the churro vendor. He never could resist a churro. And in his defense, it's not like you can just get them any time. You gotta jump on a churro opportunity when it's available.

"Two churros please," he said.

The vendor reached into the glass case and grabbed a hot churro with a piece of wax paper.

"Wait a minute," said Trapper. "What are you doing here?" He realized the blonde working the churro cart was the same one who had delivered the snow globes to him . . . well, two snow globes to him and one to Judy Ravioli.

As the snow globe courier/churro vendor lifted the churro, it caught the edge of the blonde wig and knocked it off.

Trapper's eyes became huge. "You're—hold on," he said, interrupting himself. "Let me grab this real quick." He took a huge bite out of the churro. "That's good," he said while chewing, "but don't forget, I ordered two."

The individual that was now clearly a man handed Trapper a second churro.

"You're Oakley Spice!" Trapper whisper shouted.

"Keep it down," said Oakley.

"First of all, you're a dude? I did think your shoulders were a little buff for a woman."

"Thanks. I do some training when I have time."

"Are you here to help us?"

"No."

"So, you're a double agent?"

"No."

"Well, what then? Why were you involved in the snow globe deals?"

"Well, you know I'm pretty connected. I used to be a billionaire and all. And I was running in the same circles as your dad when he visited Europe. So, this mutual friend of ours, Damien—this guy is a real charmer, by the way. I'm telling you, he texts us the best memes of all time. I mean, *ridiculous* memes." He smiled as a few of Damien's classics popped into his mind. "So anyway, Damien needed me to get the snow globes to your dad."

"That's weird. The Big Cheese told me the snow globes were being traded for favors with world leaders. That's more my bag. He never mentioned Damien being involved in this. Damien's just a top-shelf playboy like me," Trapper said as he wiped a clump of cinnamon and sugar off his chin with his forearm.

"World leaders are involved; it's just being coordinated by Damien—whether they realize it or not. By the way, sorry about how MacDonald ended up with the third snow globe. That's my bad."

"Hey, don't be hard on yourself. I was late that day because I went back for seconds at a Mongolian barbecue I hit near the Great Wall. In retrospect, I shouldn't have stopped off there when we had an appointment. But that food was so tasty."

"It's all good."

"So, why are you here?" Trapper said as he devoured half of churro number two with one bite.

"I spent so much on Fluttyr . . . turned out to be a real financial drain." He held up his phone with his company's app loaded. "I'm just here to live-flit whatever the hell is going on between your dad and MacDonald to try to drive some traffic our way. If we don't pull the company back into the black by the end of this fiscal year, I'm going to lose a bundle."

"Well, I'm gonna have to tell my dad what you've shared with me about Damien. That sounds fishy."

"Are you sure you have to tell him?" said Oakley as he waved a third churro in the air.

Trapper turned his head and saw his dad and MacDonald getting close to each other in the distance. Then looked back to Oakley. "You drive a hard bargain, Spice." He swiped the churro and took a bite.

Oakley held up his phone with an unspoken request for a selfie. Trapper obliged, stopping chewing long enough to smile, though his cheeks were still stuffed with churro.

Oakley flitted their selfie as the two made their way toward the presidential action.

Hyden and MacDonald stopped walking, leaving about five feet between them.

"That looks like President Hyden," Flynn said as he peered from behind the fence. "And is that—"

Klaven began whistling "Scotland the Brave."

"Yep, the Scot," said Jordache. "Well, the American of Scottish descent who happens to be the former President of the United States. Ace MacDonald."

"What in the world is he doing here? And how did Klaven know?"

Klaven nodded at his friend in white.

"Like you three, he is battling for the fate of humanity," said Ángel, "whether he knows it or not."

"What's with the bowling pin, Moe? I didn't come here to play games," said MacDonald.

"It's a hollowed-out compartment in the shape of a bowling pin. You can hide stuff inside, like one of those fake soda cans. A gift from my wife I've been looking for a way to unload. I love to bowl, but I mean, this thing is ridiculous. Anyway, my resignation letter is inside. I figured you could keep the pin as a trophy."

"Alright, Moe." MacDonald reached into his bowling bag and pulled out the snow globe. He tucked it between his elbow and side and extended his free arm. "Hand it over."

"You first, Ace. I know you fight dirty, and I need that snow globe."

Demons came flying out of the JFK museum and posted up as if seated at a stadium surrounding the two Presidents.

The Presidents—and all the other humans in attendance, and all humans around the world—had the most odd expression overtake their faces. It was probably a look that had never occurred on a human face before.

Eppy, Von Cappuccino, and OAC emerged from the old Book Depository building. Their mission accomplished, they had discarded their Antifa/ninja costumes and now wore loose-fitting, white, cult-membery clothing. They walked arm-in-arm, with a dopey, self-pleased look on their faces, singing their theme song, quite off-key thanks to OAC. *"Envision all the masses . . ."* They had now achieved the tripartite leftist dream they were convinced would produce paradise on Earth: They made all humans one race; they forced financial equity across the globe; and now, in their most bizarre feat, tapping into biology, chemistry, physics, and demonically influenced technology, they used Tesla's great towers to turn all of humanity into one sexless gender. I'll spare you the details. Just think Barbie and Ken but with a simple, single-purpose means of excreting liquid waste. And nothing else.

MacDonald reached down and grabbed his crotch. He fell to his knees. The snow globe dropped from his hands and landed in the grass. "No! The greatest loss to humanity of all time has just occurred!"

Jordache and Flynn looked at each other speechless. Klaven and Ángel both shrugged.

Most people were in a state of shock as they contemplated the meaning of this latest, stupefying development.

But the strangest reaction occurred in Raven DiCherubino. Zer life was built on using zer hatred for humanity to provoke discord. Zhe stirred up fights in the sandbox as a toddler, pitting one child against another through accusations and innuendo. Zhe triangulated in ever-shifting alliances in zer home as a teen, turning zer siblings and parents into hostile antagonists in zer twisted melodrama. Zhe chased that emotional viper of enmity into adulthood and stoked racial hatred between people with Z'Bendy. And hatred between people who made different amounts of money. And between people of different sexes and sexual attractions. And now, with race, class, and sex removed as means by which to produce further venom between people, zhe became a spiritual black hole of hate. The demons tried to cling to each other, for they had been through this before and felt it to be quite an unpleasant experience, but they had no chance due to their irresistible attraction to evil. All accursed spirits gathered for the spectacle in Dealey Plaza were sucked into DiCherubino's void.

A manic frenzy exploded within zer as zhe launched onto Z'Bendy, the yin to zer yang, in a ferocious assault.

Meanwhile, Hyden, though aghast about his neutering, was still a man . . . well, a person . . . on a mission, and he saw this as his opportunity. He tightened his grip on the hollowed-out bowling pin and whacked MacDonald—who was still on the ground weeping—in the head.

If the pin had been solid, MacDonald might have been taken out of the game. But a hollow pin hitting that thick Scottish skull just put him into a stupor. Judy Ravioli and The Scribe raced to his side and inspected his injury.

"Should we intervene?" asked Jordache.

Ángel put his open hand up, implying that they should not.

Hyden picked up the snow globe and watched as the day's first sunbeam entered the glass and bent upward, revealing the evil delight on his face. He staggered to the sidewalk and dashed the globe into the concrete below.

Retrieved the scroll from the tiny banana and put it in his pocket.

"I thought you loved snow globes," said MacDonald as he wobbled to his feet.

"I did, Ace, but I love power more."

"Look," said Jordache. For as far as she and Flynn and Klaven and Ángel could see, tulips opened before them into a blossom world, petals peeling back from the heavens above as if to embrace the soft sunshine of dawn. "If there was no purpose to the tulips beyond this . . . field of hope . . . it was worth it."

"Speak for yourself," said Flynn. "Though I will admit, they do look beautiful."

MacDonald walloped Hyden square in the mouth.

Hyden touched his face and saw blood on his hand. He looked at the Secret Service. "What are you waiting for, you idiots?"

A warm smile overtook MacDonald's face. "Mornin', fellas," he said to the Secret Service. "I really missed you guys."

The lead Secret Service agent put his hand to his forehead in a salute. "We missed you, too, sir." And with that, the six of them turned on their heels, military style, so they were facing the opposite direction, making it clear that Hyden would be on his own for this battle. They split up into groups of two and entered the streets to block any morning traffic that might be coming to life with the start of the day.

Hyden grabbed the bowling pin and lifted it up to give MacDonald another whack. Suddenly the lights went out as Judy Ravioli stuck the bowling ball bag over Hyden's head. She leaped onto his back, giving valiant but pretty weak slaps to the President's shoulders.

MacDonald got one good punch into Hyden's breadbasket, but then he found himself in a similar situation with Blasé stuck to his back, swatting his shoulders in some kind of doggy-paddle attack that annoyed rather than achieved damage.

"Are you getting all of this, Scribe?" shouted MacDonald.

"Of course, sir," said The Scribe as he detailed the bedlam he observed on a roll of double-ply tissue.

Spice tapped away on his phone, adding abbreviated descriptions to the photos and videos he live-flitted.

DiCherubino gave Z'Bendy a savage headbutt to the jaw, which knocked him out.

OAC led the stooges into a second round of "Envision," as they now stood a few yards from the action.

Hyden, Ravioli, MacDonald, and Blasé stumbled into the street. With two of them being in their late seventies and the other two lacking any physical vitality, despite their younger ages, it was a pretty feeble brawl.

But then Ravioli got a good cat scratch in across Hyden's cheek, giving MacDonald an opening. "Take that, you SOB," he said as he landed a devastating knee into the President's thigh. The audible crack of Hyden's femur bone made all four of them cringe.

Hyden fell to the ground in the street, panting, sweating, and groaning in agony. He tried to move forward with his one good leg and two arms, but it was no use. "Trapper!"

Trapper dropped the wax paper from his recently completed churro. He hustled to his dad's side as Blasé distracted MacDonald and Ravioli. Blasé did the ol' "fists curving toward himself while spinning them in circles like an old-timey boxer" maneuver. "Put 'em up, put 'em up," he said, but then he would jump backward when they got close to him.

"Where have you been?" Hyden said to his son.

"You wouldn't believe this. I ran into Oakley Spice, and then there were these churros—"

"Never mind," said Hyden. "I need you to do something very important. You can't screw this up!" he shouted. He reached into his pocket and pulled out the four scrolls. "Get these to the sixth floor of that building," he said pointing to the old Book Depository. There is a man there who will enter this code into his computer. It is time for THE GREAT EXCHANGE!"

"Got it, Big Cheese."

As Trapper scurried off with the scrolls, the diesel engine of a livestock truck could be heard pulling into the parking lot behind Jordache, Flynn, Klaven, and Ángel. It was Noah. He hopped out of the truck.

"Here," he said reaching out his hand with a flash drive. "You're going to have to get this to the computer on the sixth floor of the Book Depository. Don't let anyone stop you."

"What do we do once we get it into the computer?" said Jordache.

"Don't worry. Klaven knows what to do."

The corners of Flynn's mouth pinched with skepticism. "Klaven knows what to do? I don't know about that. You better come with us, Noah."

"Something I need to take care of out here."

Klaven took the flash drive, and they were off.

Blyx, trapped in torment in DiCherubino, saw Jordache and her crew and realized that whatever they were up to could foil all of his plans. He had to speed things up, so he summoned his colleagues' attention. "You know what to do!"

A few demons grumbled. "I know this is evil and all," said one, "but it's always so gross."

And without further ado, DiCherubino, in a demonically-powered act, began to consume Z'Bendy in one very slow, swallowing gulp.

Jordache and company were horrified as they approached the disgusting scene.

"Is that Raven DiCherubino *eating* Abe Z'Bendy, B.S.?" said Jordache, as they raced toward the Book Depository.

"I think so," said Flynn.

"Remember when we were talking here months ago, and I said there were three things the Left would do now that race was gone?"

"You said they'll divide and conquer, attack their opponents, and you never got to the third thing."

Jordache looked at Flynn as they ran. "That third thing was that will devour their own, though I most certainly imagined that being a figurative meal."

139

Flynn stuck his tongue out like he was going to be sick.

Trapper arrived at the sixth floor of the Book Depository first, as he had a head start. He did stop to grab one more churro, but he still reached Anonymous before the others found their way to the building's entrance.

"Hey, I need you to enter this code into your computer," he said.

Anonymous was standing, putting on his sweater.

"I just clocked out. Come back tomorrow morning. Tourists will be arriving soon."

"The Big Cheese needs this done now!"

"The Great Exchange?"

"That's right."

A big sigh. "Fine," said Anonymous. He took his sweater off and waived his fingertips toward himself with irritation.

Trapper handed him the scrolls. "Looks like a bunch of gobbledygook to me. Cool mask, by the way."

"Thanks. Had it custom-made on Etsy." Anonymous laid the scrolls out on his desk. "Ah, the ol' multi-layer puzzle completion code. Classic," he said with a nerdy chuckle. He stacked the scrolls a few different ways until one combination produced a series of exotic, but graphically complete, symbols. He unplugged his keyboard and placed it aside. Reached into his European man bag, pulled out a keyboard with symbols like those on the scroll, and plugged it into his computer. Navigated to GreatExchange.com. X'd out the warning that read,

"Abandon all hope, ye who enter here." And started typing in the code.

The door popped open.

"I told you. Probably a tour of school kids."

"Wrong," said Jordache. "We need that computer. Now!"

Anonymous picked up the pace of his typing, ignoring Jordache.

Across the world, in a European castle, Damien sat at a computer. He was surrounded by legions of demons and Satan himself, watching as the code Anonymous typed materialized on his screen.

"Is it really my big moment?" said Satan, letting an emotional whimper slip out as he spoke. A tear dropped from his eye and sizzled to steam on his cheek. He looked at Zyzyx and Slin, who were fighting back a snicker. "I'm not crying, you're crying," the pathetic Devil snapped at them.

"Stop typing!" shouted Jordache. Flynn approached Trapper, as if to fight, but then thrust a churro he had been holding behind his back just below the glutton's nose.

Trapper took the churro and walked off.

"Well, here goes nothing," said Anonymous as he lifted his hand over the enter button. He slammed his finger down and let out a self-satisfied huff.

Damien, Satan, and the castle full of demons sat on the edge of their seats. Satan, laughing, spread his wings. "We are finally ready to take over the world. He'll rule as the Antichrist," he said, pointing at Damien, "I'll rule him. It's going to be far out." Satan never could fully let go of the 1960s lingo. That's the era when he really thought he gained some momentum.

But then nothing happened.

"What are they waiting for?" cried Satan. "Maybe the WI-FI isn't working. The reception in these castles is always horrible. Why isn't that fool checking his router?" he said, directing his angst at Damien.

Anonymous looked at the computer, confused by the stalled transmission. "But I hit 'enter.' That should have delivered control of The Grid to AI," he said, now slamming 'enter' over and over in a rapid attack of his cooky keyboard. He looked down and saw a grinning Klaven, who held in his hand the keyboard cord he had just unplugged. "Guess again," said the Gypsy. He reached up and pulled off Anonymous's Guy Fawkes mask.

"Willy Dørs?!" said Jordache.

Flynn was in disbelief. "The Founder of the MacroHard Dørs operating system is . . . Anonymous?"

"Well not anymore," said Willy, "not since this jerk here took my mask off and exposed my identity. I would have gotten away with it, too, if it weren't for you meddling kids."

"And you claimed to be a philanthropist?" said Klaven.

"Try philanthro*fist*," said Dørs as he brought his girlish hand back in a windup.

"Save the Klaven!" screamed Jordache.

Flynn reached up and easily caught Dørs's fist in its effeminate thrust forward.

Klaven gave a forceful nudge to Dørs to move him out of the way and then plugged the regular keyboard back into the computer. He deleted the code Dørs had entered just to be safe.

Satan's black heart pulsated in disappointment as each symbol, one by one, vanished from Damien's screen.

Damien quickly lost interest, loaded the Macarena video into his browser, and started dancing.

"Thad," said Satan as he looked at Damien with disgust. "He's no use to us now."

"True," said Thad in his typical bootlicker tone. "What do you want us to do to him? Drive him insane? Cause a little accident, if you know what I mean?"

"Oh," Satan stomped his foot, "give him, like, a really bad cold sore, and make sure everyone can see it. One that is right at the corner of his mouth so each time he opens and closes his mouth, it really hurts." And with that, Satan dashed out of the room to a safe space at a local university where there were plenty of stuffed toys and coloring books and lots of tissues for his bitter tears.

Dørs shoved his weird code keyboard into his European man bag and stomped off toward the door. "The Secret Society doesn't provide me with enough degenerate private island perks for this."

A group of school kids on the first tour of the day passed him on the way in. "You're wasting your time," he snipped. "The museum tour's lame."

"That's an offensive, ableist thing to say, mister," said a little ten-year-old.

"Oh . . . shut up! And, you misgendered me, by the way. Apparently, we're all one gender now!"

Another little kid kicked him in the shin, and he hobbled out of the room, throwing his Guy Fawkes mask on the ground as he exited.

Klaven put the flash drive Noah gave him in the computer. The view shifted from the MacroHard Dørs user-friendly screen to an old-school screen with a flashing green cursor. Klaven's fingers moved so fast they were a blur to Jordache and Flynn.

He hit enter, and the screen became a cascade of code.

"You're a . . . computer programmer?" said Flynn. "Why didn't you tell us?"

"You never asked," said Klaven as he put his hands behind his head and propped his feet up on the desk. Signature grin in place, he watched the data flow by. "It was getting hard to be a Gypsy, so I learned to code."

"What exactly is happening here?" asked Jordache.

"Oh, no big deal," said Klaven in his sing-songy delivery. "Just taking control back from the Deep Deep State, which was on the verge of handing over all computing power of the world to AI. It's also restoring the financial records that existed before Equity occurred. And removing the virus that equalizes all bank deposits."

"And all that, all the financial records in existence, are on that little flash drive?" Flynn said in a challenge to Klaven.

"There's no way to store that much data on a flash drive," said Klaven. "You really should take a course in computer science, Flynn."

"Funny," he said. "So, what is on the flash drive?"

"The Sons of Thunder had been working around the clock to develop a way to infiltrate the coding of the Deep Deep State's operation. But they had to wait for the Deep Deep State to finish integrating the global computing systems, which they refer to as 'The Grid.' Well, they must have completed The Grid while we were in the gardens early this morning, which allowed the Sons of Thunder to send their code to us." Klaven pointed at the flash drive. "The code on that is redirecting The Grid to the servers at Gopherwood Farm. We've been staying in the day-to-day ops level below the farm. But there's a vast underground warehouse below that with more servers than you can shake a tulip at. By about right now," Klaven said looking at his broken watch, then at the computer screen which had returned to a single flashing cursor, "The Sons of Thunder have commandeered the system. Once they restore the financial data that existed before Equity, they will then redistribute that data across a variety of networks. They're using blockchain technology to ensure it is dispersed and protected against centralized control, including AI—for now. It's complicated, but Noah assembled the top programmers in the world at his *data farm*," he said with an exaggeratedly deadpan delivery.

"How do you know all this?" asked Jordache.

"While you two were meeting with Noah every day, I was hanging out by the programmers' water cooler. That's where you get all the good dirt. They all love you, by the way," he said to Jordache. "You," he turned to Flynn, "they weren't so sure about you at first, but you grew on them. A little."

"Thanks for sharing that, Klaven," said Flynn.

Jordache turned to Ángel. "So, the mission is to undo the bizarre phenomena that have been happening of late. The civilizational Jungian shadow reared its ugly head via these corrupt totalitarian utopianists, and we are now integrating the shadow back into the collective unconscious?"

"No," said Ángel. "No offense, but that sounds like a bunch of psychobabble."

"None taken."

"The reality is, humans entrusted with social and political power invited evil to overtake their hearts." He shook his head in disappointment. "But the true shame is that so many people were too cowardly to simply object to this evil, even when their own children's innocence and goodness was under attack. They've been lulled into complacency and spiritual blindness by the comfort of affluence." The others noticed that Ángel's skin began to shimmer. "But He," he said, lifting his eyes heavenward, "in His wisdom and grace, did not consider it time for the Apocalypse yet. So here we are."

"Ah," said Jordache, speaking to a being whose skin now appeared to be more light than flesh. "Fair enough. So, I take it you're an actual angel."

"C'mon, guys. Wasn't it obvious? I mean, the immaculate garments, the prophecies, *my name*?" Ángel shared a chuckle with Klaven. "See you all when it's your time." And with that, he disappeared in a flash of white light.

Jordache, Flynn, and Klaven all felt as if they were floating in the afterglow of Ángel's exit.

As the elation faded, the relaxed look on Jordache's face tightened to focused. "We should go see what's happening between Hyden and MacDonald."

Children continued to enter the room as part of their tour.

"Aren't you kids here a little early in the day?" said Flynn as the three made their way to the door.

Their pink-haired teacher piped up. "We're an elite private school. We're on New York time."

"That figures."

Klaven stooped down to the kids' level. "The CIA did it," he said and then jogged to catch up to Jordache and Flynn.

"It was a lone shooter driven by white supremacy!" the teacher bellowed behind them.

Jordache, Flynn, and Klaven approached the grassy knoll area, which was now surrounded by a large crowd making odd sighs and groans of disgust.

Flynn gave friendly elbows to clear a path through the crowd for his wife and begrudgingly for Klaven.

"You know," Jordache said, "I wish I would have asked Ángel what the circle meant, the one he drew in the air when he was still in prison."

147

"Apparently, he was making the sign of the ouroboros, the snake that consumes itself," said Klaven as he lifted his finger to point. His grin was replaced by a grimace. "Some have tried to give the ouroboros a positive meaning, but I think we can put that to rest."

Jordache and Flynn looked up—

. . . Past the brawling Presidents. The nearly octogenarians were almost completely out of juice. Hyden was reduced to giving a faint noogie to MacDonald's heel, while MacDonald delivered equally innocuous blows to Hyden's head with the hollowed-out bowling pin.

. . . Past Judy Ravioli and Panderson Blasé, who now sat on the curb, panting and brushing dust off themselves. They bowed out of the scuffle when they realized their expensive clothing was getting disheveled.

. . . Past Oakley Spice, who continued to live-flit the debacle. His eyebrows were raised so high they were about to lift right off his head.

Jordache, Flynn, and Klaven looked past all of that and saw Raven DiCherubino reduced to zer core of pure hatred. Zhe had already, with the supernatural actions of the tormented and demented souls within zer, completely devoured Z'Bendy.

Now directly on top of the white "X" in the street marking the spot where JFK was assassinated, zhe looked out at the crowd through the eyes of a depraved beast.

"There is only one way out now," said Blyx to his damned comrades, "and that is through!"

148

All gathered watched as DiCherubino began to devour zerxelf, as the ouroboran snake is depicted in ancient drawings, tail, or in zer case feet, first.

"Above us solely air," sang the stooges as DiCherubino gulped the last bite of zerxelf and disappeared.

Standing off to the side was Noah with a knowing look on his face and several dozen pigs on the ground around him. "And the mouth of the wicked devoureth iniquity."

Blyx and his horde of demons lunged into the pigs, and the possessed pigs ran off in search of a cliff.

"He catches the wise in their own craftiness, and the schemes of the wily are brought to a quick end," sang Klaven.

Flynn looked at him. "Zeppelin?"

"Book of Job."

Flynn nodded. "Ah."

Jordache put her hands on her hips and looked at the spot that a moment before hosted one of the most revolting horrors ever witnessed. "Well. That was weird."

Denouement

It was hard to shock people after The Great Race Blender, Equity, and what came to be called Neutergeddon. But it was still something to see a human devour zerxelf. The crowd stood still, trying to understand what it had just witnessed.

One man moved forward.

It was Oakley Spice. He approached MacDonald and Hyden, who were still in their odd position of Hyden at MacDonald's foot. "Fight's over, fellas," said Spice, holding his phone up for both to see.

Noah's programmers had been doing more than backing up computer data, it turns out. One of their many other tasks was to tap into the recording system of the White House. It was like the one Nixon used to tape his conversations but digital. They captured every bowling lane conversation with Hyden, Raven DiCherubino, Abe Z'Bendy, B.S., Panderson Blasé, and Trapper. And they uploaded it all to Fluttyr.

"Game over, Hyden," said Spice as they listened to Hyden lay out his plot to hand over control of the world to AI and Damien.

Blasé heard his voice in the recordings. He tiptoed backward and slinked away from the scene.

"But you were at The Secret Society meetings, too, Oakley," said Hyden.

"Hey, I was just there on a guest pass. I never joined."

MacDonald stood up. He opened the bowling pin and pulled out the letter Hyden had said was inside.

"You actually did include a resignation letter."

"Even gangsters live by a code," said Hyden. "Plus, I was giving up the Presidency to be a god-king, so I thought it was hilariously ironic to write up an actual resignation letter."

"Not so fast, Moe," said MacDonald, "You didn't sign it." He pulled a pen out of his pocket. It was one of the cheap giveaway pens with his name on it from his leg warmer days. "You know the routine," he said, bending down and handing Hyden the pen.

"Lower," said Hyden. "I can't move because of my leg."

MacDonald crouched as low as he could so Hyden could use his back like a desk, as he did so many years ago in the alley behind Big Al's Car Shack.

"Here," said Hyden, lifting his resignation. "This pen is crap, by the way."

MacDonald carefully read Hyden's letter and then held it up for those gathered to see. Spice flitted a photo of it.

"Yay. This means I'm President again," said MacDonald.

"Not so fast, sir," said Spice. He scrolled on his phone to a live stream flit coming from the White House. They watched as a woman spoke from the President's desk in the Oval Office.

"Vice President Lotus Sparus!" shouted MacDonald. "Gotta be honest. I totally forgot about her."

"Live from the White House, it's the Lotus Sparus Show," she said before her voice exploded into a ridiculous cackle. "Oh, we're on the air. Okay, okay," she said, trying to compose herself. She looked into the camera. "My fellow Americans, we have been closely following the grave events of Dealey Plaza today, including the exposure of President Hyden's corruption," she said, not quite holding back a grin. "Thankfully, President Hyden did not trust me due to my—his words, not mine—'incompetence,' so I was completely uninvolved in all of his unfortunate dealings, which I fully disavow. We watched former President Hyden sign his resignation letter moments ago on Fluttyr, and I just happen to always have the Chief Justice of the Supreme Court on standby because I'm looking out for you . . . He just swore me in. Had my hand on Mao's Little Red Book and everything." She couldn't hold back her cackle anymore, speaking and laughing at the same time. "And now I'd like to introduce to you, me, President Lotus Sparus. I like the sound of that. It's like the Venn Diagram of power and me overlapping in the middle."

"Enough of that, Spice," said MacDonald. "A woman devouring herself before our very eyes is one thing, but that cackle. It's too much. It really is. Thankfully, we do have an election coming up, and my poll numbers have been through the roof ever since I was wrongly convicted and sent to GITMO. That cackling fraud's days are numbered."

Jordache, Flynn, and Klaven approached and introduced themselves to MacDonald. They explained their role in removing the Deep Deep State's control of The Grid.

"Can you at least get me a doctor?" said Hyden, pointing to his leg, which was painful to look at given that it had an extra bend in it. "I think I'm going into shock."

"We'll get to you," said MacDonald. "But there's something much, much more pressing. What can we do about this?" he said, motioning to his groin area.

Just then, a breeze passed over Dealey Plaza, across the garden of tulips, and into the lungs of those gathered. It turned out there was a naturally occurring chemical in tulips that counteracted the unisex component of the stooges' Envision Protocol. Blyx wasn't the only one monitoring and coordinating with scientists. Ángel had quite a network, too—not to mention direct access to the Creator of the cosmos. And as the chemical worked its way through the bloodstreams and into the brains of those gathered, well—everything began to fall back into its right place, if you know what I mean.

MacDonald's face took on a peculiar shape. His eyebrows gathered in the middle of his forehead. His lips contracted into an odd pucker. His eyes narrowed from the top and sides. And then all released into a soft euphoria.

He smiled. "Little Ace is back, folks—all is well!"

A similar reaction occurred for all who were gathered. Anatomically and emotionally. Well, at least for most of them.

The chemical reaction reached the nether regions of Eppy, Von Cappuccino, and OAC. They finally stopped singing that tired John Beetle tune.

"To be honest," said Von Cappuccino with a forceful release of air, "I was experiencing some post-transition regret."

"Same here," said Eppy. "Do you have any kombucha?"

"Yeah, back at my hotel."

"Let's get out of here," said Eppy as the two walked off.

OAC, however, crouched awkwardly in her white outfit. "My communist dream is over," she wept with great sorrow.

Even though Spice was mainly known for beer koozies and being the owner of Fluttyr, he was also pretty good at sciencey stuff. "If I had to guess, I'd say the return of our sex organs is related to these tulips that have, serendipitously enough, been planted everywhere."

Word would spread quickly that tulips were the antidote for Neutergeddon. People of the world raced posthaste to their local botanical gardens to inhale some tulip excretions. Everyone was so glad to have their full bodies back that even Antifa called a cease-fire on their attacks on straight men. They tore up their photos of Olivia Newton-John, which they found to be icky, and put down their bars of prison-issue soap. They were never that into soap in the first place, so that part was easy.

"I've got to ask you, President MacDonald," said Flynn.

"Please, call me Ace. By the way, I used to watch *The Cocky Crowe Show* before it got canceled. Loved your white guy impression."

"Oh, well, thanks, Ace. I did an impression of you, too. People tell me it was a tremendous impression, the best really," he said impersonating MacDonald.

"Yeah. Wasn't a fan of that. At all."

"Right. So, like I was saying, Ace, what's with the teardrop tattoo? Did you, uh, shank someone in prison, or what?"

"It's much worse than that, really. The guards at GITMO showed us the film *Marley & Me* on movie night. Tore me up, Flynn. It just tore me up. That dog gave so much love. I really don't like to talk about it," he said with a sniffle.

The Secret Service entered the grassy knoll area and played a round of Rock, Paper, Scissors. The losers had to take Hyden to the hospital, while the other three walked off with MacDonald.

The crowd slowly dispersed, leaving Jordache, Flynn, and Klaven sitting alone on the grassy knoll.

Jordache pulled a can of tuna out of her purse and peeled off the lid. The three took turns eating the tuna, sharing her single spoon.

"Just to be clear," said Flynn, "it turns out Equity was worse than anyone could have even imagined. Any more of that, and we all would've starved by year's end."

"Not to mention, there would have been no more humans after this generation without sexual differences anyway," said Klaven.

"Well, hopefully, these vacuums of intelligence have learned that it's foolish to try to force us to all be the same," said Jordache. "And woe to those who attempt to divide us based on our differences. It's like, the ouroboros is no joke. And don't think it couldn't be you next time, princess."

"Which one of us are you calling princess, anyway?" said Klaven.

"She's speaking rhetorically," said Flynn. "Just listen. She's riffing. That's when she really shines."

"You get sloppy," Jordache continued. "Avoid a necessary sacrifice that will benefit your future self. Allow yourself to, oh, let's say, entertain a resentment, *hmm*? Tell a lie and cling to it like bloody hell until a pit of hatred grows in you that's deeper and darker than you can imagine. We saw a glimpse of that today."

"More of a glimpse than I would ever want to see," said Flynn.

"That's for damn sure," said Jordache. "Life's hard. It's not fair. Vipers abound at every turn, especially in the cracks and crevices and under the rocks you forgot to check. So, buck up, buttercup, it's gonna be a wild ride. Anchor your life in the truth and love that emanates from God—if you dare contemplate what that means. Exhibit a little courage, even if you think you don't have it. Develop some damn grit. Then, and only then, you just might find your life being flooded with meaning and beauty so intense that you will pass through the tragedy and heartache and tribulation which will come your way and survive to help someone else do the same. And the waves of this feral world—the ones that bash into each other in what most hear as a cacophony—will for you harmonize into a sublime melody of life, a song that unites you in bliss with the Father of lights."

The tuna can made its way to Klaven. "*Mmm,*" he said as he took a bite. "Salty. Just like the tears of my vanquished enemies."

"You know, Klaven," said Flynn, "Noah was right. You get it."

And the three looked out pleased, basking in the view of thousands of glorious tulips, red petals lifting upward in plant praise.

• • •

Well, that about wraps things up.

Trapper was on round three of an all-you-can-eat breakfast buffet around the corner from Dealey Plaza when the authorities arrested him for his part in the attempted Great Exchange. Local authorities that is. The feds were corrupt, and it would take years into Ace's next Presidential term before the federal agencies were reformed. MacDonald tasked his chief advisor Judy Ravioli with cleaning up the Deep State as well as the

Deep Deep State, a never-ending job, but she made progress. Lots of undercover costumes for Ravioli. And lots of bad accents.

President MacDonald had the golden calf melted down and sold. The revenue was used to pay for a tulip garden in every city in the country as a memorial to the day that Little Ace, and everyone else's Little Aces and Ace-ettes, too, so to speak, returned. Ace tended to focus on the crude, but it was truly a worthy moment, as it made survival for humanity possible again.

He also reinstituted paper currency. "If the piles of thousand dollar bills I roll around in on my bed every night have no real value, what's the fun? I hereby announce that cash is back, baby!"

People's races stayed the same. Ángel could have reversed that while he helped humans undo the other two changes of the Envision Protocol, but race doesn't matter, so he left it alone. Naturally, people found plenty of other things to be jerks about.

And Blyx?

He received his final, just reward . . . well, final reward before the Judgment, that is . . .

After a good long cry in the university's safe space, Satan called a meeting of the World Demonic Forum to do some damage control.

"Just to reiterate, it was not my idea to call forth the Antichrist at this time. This was all on you, Blyx."

Blyx Zümed into the meeting. All could see that the ambitious spark was gone from his eye after what, for the demonic realm, was a complete fiasco. Satan was furious, of course, but all of the demons who had to exit DiCherubino via the ouroboros maneuver were still miffed. Not to mention, much of the evil other demons had been working on was undone. Amping up animosity based on race, class, and gender to the point of absurdity actually had the unintended effect of waking more people up to the reality that they were being manipulated.

"Here's what I'm thinking," the embattled demon said. "We try to keep people separated into different geographic regions. That way, over time, skin colors will likely change again, then we can—"

Satan slammed his fist on the table. "Enough! This guy just doesn't know when to stop," he said, looking at Thad.

"I know, right?" Thad was quick to reply.

"That would take hundreds of thousands of years if it worked at all!" boomed Satan. "I'm all about immediate gratification."

"You blew it so bad," Zyzyx said looking at Blyx, "it was almost like you were trying to make things . . . good."

"Exactly," said Satan. "I mean, the humans realized that forced equity will destroy them. We lost race as a divisive weapon. Child gender mutilations are banned worldwide now—in no small part thanks to your bungling of your own plan, which I was skeptical about from the start, right?" Satan looked around to get nods of approval from the yes-demons at the table. "So now, you are hereby permanently exiled to the heinous region in which you stand—the place where the extremes of self-indulgence and smugness are overwhelming even to a fiend. *Mooahh hah hah hah hah!*"

The demons delighted as their Züm view of Blyx panned out to reveal he had been banished to . . . San Francisco.

"Anything but that! Nooooooo!" the demon shrieked as the light from the screen shrank down to a dot and then, along with Blyx, disappeared.

THE END

Mx. Raven DiCherubino's Handy Dandy Personal Pronoun Guide*

πü≈ (expressed as if one is gagging): you
πü≈r (expressed as if one is gagging and adding "r"): your
πü≈'re (expressed as if one is gagging and adding "re"): you're
let'x: let's
xe: me
xeverywyne: everyone
Xi: I
xine: mine
xy: my
xyxelf: myself
ze: we
zeach xother: each other
zeir: their
ze'll: we'll
zer: her
ze're: we're
zerxelf: herself
ze've: we've
zey: they
zhe: she
zour: our
zourxelves: ourselves
zux: us

*Note: This is a glossary of Mx. DiCherubino's pronouns appearing in *No Hell Below Zux*, but it is by no means exhaustive.

Benediction

"May the Lord direct your hearts to the love of God and to the perseverance of Christ."— 2 Thessalonians 3:5

Acknowledgments

Thank you to the Father of lights, the Source of every good and perfect gift from above.

Thank you to The Babylon Bee, Andrew Klavan, Steven Crowder, JP Sears, and Mark Twain for your exquisite lessons in satire.

Thank you to Jordan Peterson for your insights and grit.

About the Author

John Twain is a cowboy. Well, a pretend cowboy,
but still.

Connect

Facebook: @ShimmerTreeBooks

Twitter: @WriterJohnTwain; @TheShimmerTree

LinkedIn: ShimmerTreeBooks

https://www.shimmertreebooks.com/

shimmertreebooks@gmail.com

Shimmer Tree Books

If you enjoyed *No Hell Below Us: A Political Tour de Farce*, please help it reach more readers by leaving a review on Amazon, Goodreads, and social media. This will make a huge difference and be very much appreciated.

Thank you,
Shimmer Tree Books

Other fantastic titles from Shimmer Tree Books!

You Are a Bird is available on Amazon.

Christian Indie Awards 1st Place Winner and Winner of the Literary Titan Gold Book Award!

"*You Are a Bird* is unlike any other book I have read before. This evocative novella had so many different layers to it, that I wouldn't hesitate to heartily recommend it."

★★★★★ —Literary Titan

"The reader, regardless of age, can easily relate to his own personal, social, or cultural confinement with his dreams of the future in this philosophically probing novella, *You are a Bird*."

—AuthorsReading.com

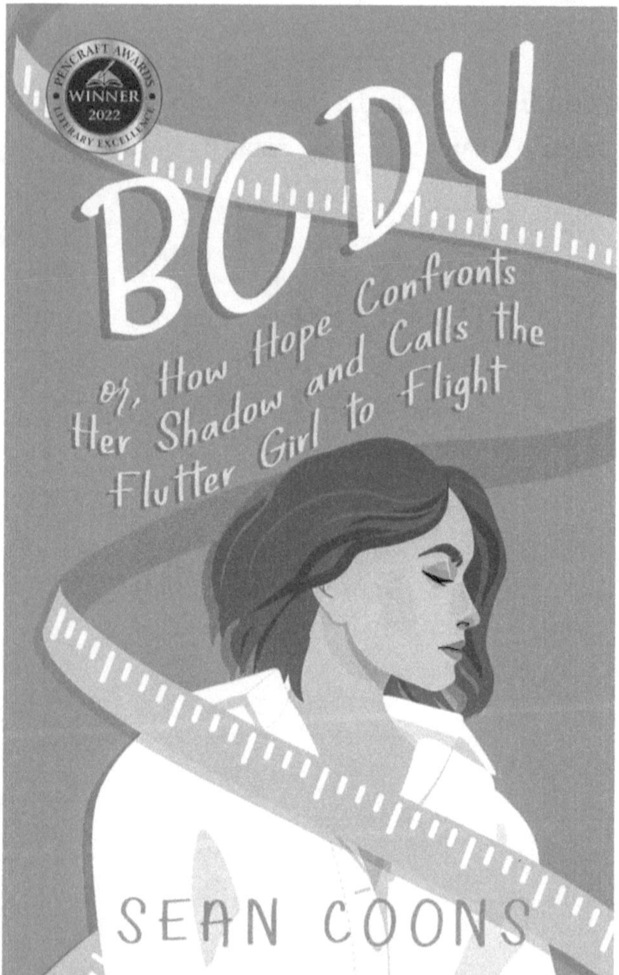
PENCRAFT AWARDS
WINNER
2022
LITERARY EXCELLENCE
BODY
or, How Hope Confronts Her Shadow and Calls the Flutter Girl to Flight
SEAN COONS

Body is available on Amazon.

Body is the Pencraft Awards Christian-Fiction Runner-Up Winner for 2022!

"This book offers truths and inspiration for any woman who's ever wondered if her body is good enough."
–Heather Creekmore, author of *Compared to Who?*

"This book made me laugh and cry as Hope works towards a better relationship with her body. It illustrates how body acceptance is better than any diet at helping a woman to feel at more peace and ease in her skin. An inspiring read for anyone struggling with their body image."
–Judi Craddock, author of *The Little Book of Body Confidence*

"This book, though written by a man, is a master class in the philosophy of female: body image, perspectives, and views."
–PJ Colando, author of *The Jailbird's Jackpot*

"I've been working on healing my relationship with food and my body, with the help of the intuitive eating framework, for several months now, but I'd got stuck. This book gave me hope and a gentle reminder that the work is necessary and will bear fruit."
–Amazon Review

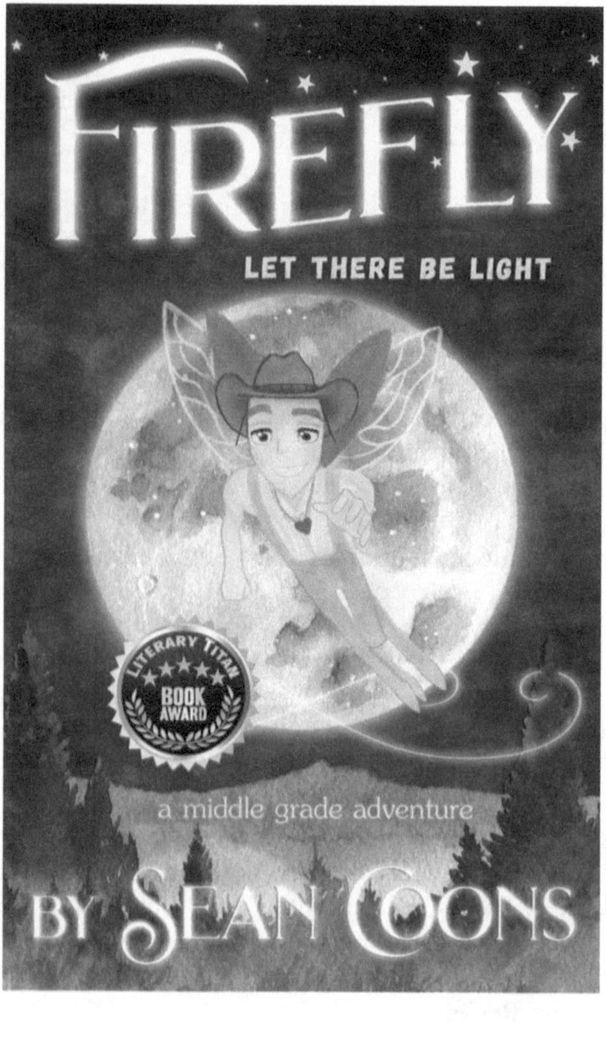
FIREFLY
LET THERE BE LIGHT
LITERARY TITAN
BOOK AWARD
a middle grade adventure
BY SEAN COONS

Firefly is available on Amazon.

Winner of the Literary Titan Gold Award!

"Filled with fatherly advice and love, this coming-of-age story is an incredible adventure with humor and words of wisdom that will delight the whole family."

★★★★★ —**Literary Titan**

"*Firefly* is a must-read, populated with endearing, flawed critters on an accidental journey that will change their lives and challenge their friendships. Sean Coons writes such beautiful prose that you will want to read it out loud just to hear the rhythms he creates with his words."
—**Patricia Beauchamp, screenwriter and producer**

"Once my 11-year-old son Trevor started reading *Firefly*, he didn't want to put it down! The story had him hooked— and not every book piques the curiosity of my adventure- focused son. Great book!"
—**Heather Creekmore, author of The Burden of Better and Compared to Who?**

"This was a great book! *Firefly* is the kind of book that makes you wish you didn't have a bedtime so you can just keep reading!"
—**Trevor Creekmore, Age 11**

SINGULARITY

or, How the LOGOS Resolves
the Problems of Racism,
Gender Obsession,
Climate Change, Decadence,
& Every Other Calamity You Encounter

by THEOPHILUS

Singularity is available on Amazon.

Called "an antidote to wokeness," *Singularity* exposes the cultural phenomena that pit people against each other in the modern world: decadence, fear of climate change, sexual and gender obsession, abortion, racism, the credibility of experts, and "divisionism." Theophilus dispels modern illusions with ancient truths in this practical yet metaphysically evocative exploration of the calamities that bombard man.

Most importantly, *Singularity* reveals how the LOGOS, Jesus Christ, resolves the chaos in your life and the world around you with divine power and love.

Shimmer Tree Books